Cynthia bit her bottom lip. "We're just friends, right?"

Cade smiled. "Right." But after kissing her… "You know what, you can have the bed. I'll sleep on the ground."

"Take the bed. I don't mind the floor."

"This is ridiculous," Cade said. "We're both adults."

"That's true." Cynthia didn't sound so confident. "It's just a b-bed."

"Exactly. Besides, I'm tired," he pointed out.

"Good, we'll both sleep." Her cheeks reddened. "I mean—"

"I know what you mean." If they were both tired, they would simply sleep. But part of him prayed that wasn't true.

Dear Reader,

We've been busy here at Silhouette Romance cooking up the next batch of tender, emotion-filled romances to add extra sizzle to your day.

First on the menu is Laurey Bright's modern-day Sleeping Beauty story, *With His Kiss* (#1660). Next, Melissa McClone whips up a sensuous, *Survivor*-like tale when total opposites must survive two weeks on an island, in *The Wedding Adventure* (#1661). Then bite into the next juicy SOULMATES series addition, *The Knight's Kiss* (#1663) by Nicole Burnham, about a cursed knight and the modern-day princess who has the power to unlock his hardened heart.

We hope you have room for more, because we have three other treats in store for you. First, popular Silhouette Romance author Susan Meier turns on the heat in *The Nanny Solution* (#1662), the third in her DAYCARE DADS miniseries about single fathers who learn the ABCs of love. Then, in Jill Limber's *Captivating a Cowboy* (#1664), are a city girl and a dyed-in-the-wool cowboy a recipe for disaster…or romance? Finally, Lissa Manley dishes out the laughs with *The Bachelor Chronicles* (#1665), in which a sassy journalist is assigned to get the city's most eligible—and stubborn—bachelor to go on a blind date!

I guarantee these heartwarming stories will keep you satisfied until next month when we serve up our list of great summer reads.

Happy reading!

Mary-Theresa Hussey
Senior Editor

The Wedding Adventure

MELISSA McCLONE

Published by Silhouette Books

America's Publisher of Contemporary Romance

To the Goalies
for their friendship, support and love.

Special thanks to Amy, Shirley and Terri
for seeing this through to the end.

SILHOUETTE BOOKS

ISBN 0-373-19661-X

THE WEDDING ADVENTURE

This edition published by arrangement with Harlequin Books S.A.

Visit Silhouette at www.eHarlequin.com

Printed in U.S.A.

Books by Melissa McClone

Silhouette Romance

If the Ring Fits… #1431
The Wedding Lullaby #1485
His Band of Gold #1537
In Deep Waters #1608
The Wedding Adventure #1661

Yours Truly

Fiancé for the Night

MELISSA MCCLONE

With a degree in mechanical engineering from Stanford University, the last thing Melissa McClone ever thought she would be doing is writing romance novels, but analyzing engines for a major U.S. airline just couldn't compete with her "happily-ever-afters."

When she isn't writing, caring for her two young children or doing laundry, Melissa loves to curl up on the couch with a cup of tea, her cats and a good book. She is also a big fan of *The X-Files* and enjoys watching home decorating shows to get ideas for her house—a 1939 cottage that is *slowly* being renovated.

Melissa lives in Lake Oswego, Oregon, with her own real-life hero husband, daughter, son, two lovable but oh-so-spoiled indoor cats and a no-longer stray outdoor kitty who decided to call the garage home. Melissa loves to hear from readers. You can write to her at P.O. Box 63, Lake Oswego, OR 97034.

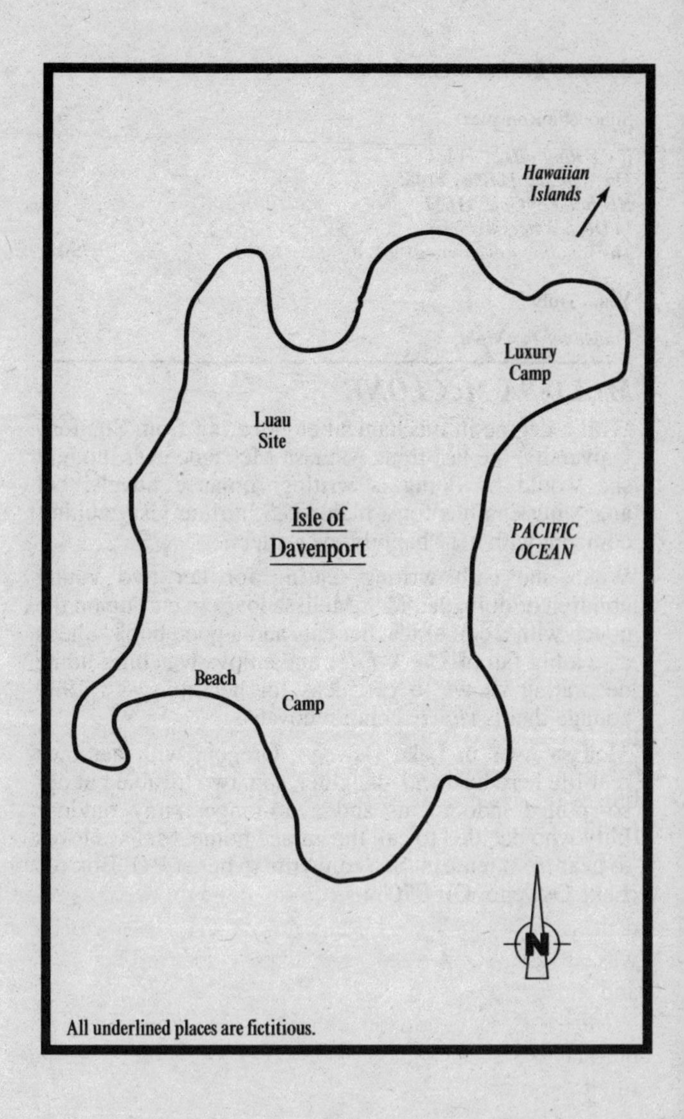
Hawaiian Islands
Luxury Camp
Luau Site
Isle of Davenport
PACIFIC OCEAN
Beach
Camp
N
All underlined places are fictitious.

Prologue

The house was too quiet.

Sitting in his library, Henry Davenport tapped his Mont Blanc pen against the top of his mahogany desk, but the floor-to-ceiling bookcases absorbed the sound. He dropped the pen and glanced around the room looking for something to do.

Dickens, Hawking, Clancy, Gardner... He wasn't in the mood to read any of the books on the shelves. His housekeeper had placed all his magazines in the recycling bin. A fire hazard was what she'd called the stack he kept by the library door.

TV wasn't an option. He'd surfed through all the cable channels and over 500 more on his three different satellite dishes. He had no shows left on his TiVo to watch. He was all caught up. And he'd already seen all his DVDs and videos.

Music. That would do the trick. He touched the play button on the CD remote. The jazzy strains of a trumpet filled the air.

Nice, but Henry wasn't in the mood for jazz. He hit another button. Vivaldi. Classical wouldn't do. Easy listening. Forget about it. Blues. Not today. Hard rock, folk, alternative, country. He made his way through the one hundred CDs stored in his player. Not one would do.

Tomorrow he'd have to buy a hundred different ones. Obviously his musical tastes had changed.

But what about now?

His Portland, Oregon, estate was deserted due to the annual retreat he sponsored for his staff. The silence had never affected Henry before, but tonight…

The quiet was a problem. He needed…something.

One phone call and he could fill the house or a club with more friends than he knew what to do with. But that wasn't what he wanted, either. It had to be something else.

The plans for his upcoming birthday party were nearly completed. All that remained was the escrow closing on the private island he'd purchased. So why did he feel as if something were missing? Something important.

Henry stared at the neat stacks of files in front of him. The invitations, the party arrangements, even the adventure. He opened the top file and studied the guest list. He'd checked and double-checked who would be joining him for an all-expense paid trip to Hawaii to attend his birthday bash on April Fools' Day. No one had been left off. He'd made certain.

The next file was about the party itself. From the catering to the live entertainment, no detail had been ignored. This year's traditional luau/tropical paradise party at one of Hawaii's most exclusive resorts was several steps up from last year's tacky wedding theme in Reno, Nevada.

Tacky or not, that party had been his best. It would be

difficult if not impossible to top Reno's success. But Henry had to try.

Each year, he threw himself a birthday party and sent two of his guests on an adventure. Every year got better, more elaborate, more fun. He thought the participants enjoyed it, too.

Maybe that was the problem. He didn't want to let his guests down. They'd come to expect certain things from him. Though none had expected him to act like Cupid.

Last year, he'd tried something new and played matchmaker with the adventure participants. The result—two of his best friends, Brett Matthews and Laurel Worthington, had fallen in love and married for real. Henry was now godfather to their almost three-month-old beautiful baby daughter, Noelle.

He stared at the half dozen pictures of Noelle on his desk and warmth surrounded his heart. He still couldn't believe someone so tiny could fill him with so much love. He couldn't wait to watch her grow, to be a part of all the milestones in her life. He already had a roomful of presents waiting for her. Everything from a life-size rocking horse to a strand of Mikamoto pearls. Bringing Noelle's parents together had been the right thing. Not only for Brett and Laurel, but Henry, too.

And that's when it hit him.

Something *was* wrong with this year's party and adventure. Something enormous. He couldn't go back to his old way of allowing fate to pick the participants. He might not be one for marriage, but he'd seen how happy Brett and Laurel were together. Henry wanted all his friends to experience the same happiness. And if he ended up with more godchildren, he wouldn't complain. Not one bit.

Excitement rushed through him. This was the feeling that had been missing. With a grin, Henry picked up his pen and studied the names on his guest list.

Who would be the next two to live happily ever after?

Chapter One

"Why did you drag me away from Travis?" Cynthia Sterling was not happy with Henry Davenport and could care less if today was his thirty-fourth birthday. "We were having such a good time."

"A good time?" Henry, wearing a green and white Hawaiian shirt and shorts, led her through the grand ballroom at one of Hawaii's top resorts. His April Fools' Day Bacchanalian birthday parties were legendary. This year's Polynesian paradise theme, complete with tiki torches illuminating the path from the tastefully decorated ballroom to the beach and luau, was no exception. Henry's customary style and taste were everywhere, not to mention the added touches—such as the beautiful and talented hula dancers—that provided local flavor. But his ever-present smile had all but disappeared. "Travis was about to drool."

She hadn't imagined that. Cynthia wet her lips. "So?"

"The man's obsessed with you, darling."

"Obsessed is such a strong word. I prefer infatuated."

"How about pathetic?" Henry suggested with a tilt of his beachcomber hat. "No matter, he'll get over it."

"Not if I can help it." Travis had the qualities she wanted in a husband. He hung on her every word, thought she could do no wrong and wanted to give her the world. "He's perfect."

"You can do better than Travis Drummond."

"What if I don't want to do better?"

"He's already jilted one bride at the altar."

"He told me," Cynthia admitted. "It wasn't his fault."

"It never is," Henry muttered.

She ignored him, glanced back and spotted a frowning Travis among the other guests. She wouldn't call him classically handsome like Henry and several of the other men in her social circle, but Travis Drummond was cute with a farm boy sort of charm, a sweet grin and a mind-boggling net worth. Like her, he was an only child. He had mentioned feeling lonely, how he wanted to settle down with the right woman and start a family. Cynthia had used every ounce of willpower to keep herself from hauling him off to a judge right then. She felt the same way. Except about finding the right woman. She needed the right man to be her husband and the father of her children.

Travis could be the one. He adored her. She liked him. What more could she want in a marriage?

His gaze met hers. He stared at her as if she were the only woman in the crowded room. In his eyes, she was and a rush of feminine power surged through her. All of her close friends were either married or engaged. She wanted the same comfort and security they had found.

Cynthia mouthed "later." Travis smiled. Maybe feeling lonely was going to be a thing of the past…for both of them.

She adjusted the hibiscus in her hair and looked up at Henry. “Travis thinks I’m the best thing he’s ever come across.”

“You are.” Henry sounded sincere, but he always said the right words. His reputation as a playboy and heart-breaker was well-earned. He oozed charm, but Cynthia was immune. He was a good friend, the closest thing she had to a big brother. She’d met him when she was a debutante and they had become fast friends despite the difference in their ages. Dating him wasn’t an option. Thcy’d tricd oncc five years ago right after she’d turned twenty-one. It felt weird, uncomfortable, wrong. They were destined to be nothing more than friends. Both were happy with that. “But before you settle on becoming Mrs. Travis Drummond, there’s someone else I want you to meet first.”

“Who?”

“Cade Waters.”

“Waters.” The name didn’t sound familiar. She knew most of the families of the rich and the eligible. “Should I know him?”

“His full name is Cade Armstrong Waters.”

She stopped walking. “Armstrong International?”

Henry nodded. “He’s one of the nephews.”

Nephew, cousin, distant relative. It didn’t matter. The Armstrongs were so wealthy they made Travis Drummond’s net worth seem like milk money. But even better was the family itself, something Travis couldn’t give her.

The Armstrongs were a large, extended family of movers and shakers who made millions and headlines. And royalty since Christina Armstrong had married His Serene Highness Prince Richard De Thierry of San Montico. A princess for a cousin-in-law. Now that would make family get-togethers interesting. Oh, family get-togethers…

Cynthia dreamed about being part of a big, loving family. She hated not having any siblings. In theory, she was part of a family. Reality, however, was another thing.

''Why haven't I heard about Cade Armstrong?'' she asked.

''Cade Armstrong Waters,'' Henry corrected. ''He keeps a low profile. Avoids the press. Some call him the black sheep of the family, but you won't meet a more perfect man.''

''I thought you were the only perfect man?''

''If only.'' Henry laughed and waved to a mutual friend. ''Cade's sister got married on Valentine's Day. You may have heard of her. Kelsey Armstrong Waters Addison.''

''Addison? As in Addison Resorts and...'' Cynthia grabbed Henry's shoulder. ''She's the wedding consultant to the stars.''

His eyes gleamed with amusement. ''Could come in handy if something developed between you and her brother?''

If something developed... The Armstrongs probably had a big Christmas gathering with a huge tree covered with lights and ornaments and a formal sit-down dinner with all the family in attendance. She could almost smell the scents of pine, vanilla and cinnamon. Almost hear the sounds of conversations, laughter and singing. A warm glow flowed through her. With Cade and the Armstrongs, she would never have to spend Christmas alone while her parents took yet another ''second'' honeymoon.

Cynthia's heart pounded. She wanted to surround herself with love, cocoon herself in a family. The Armstrongs were a ready-made one with lots of aunts and uncles and nieces and nephews and cousins. They were also rich. She would never have to worry about being poor again. This was everything she'd ever wanted and it sounded too good to be true. "Does Cade have any ex-wives, clinging ex-girlfriends or children I should know about?"

"None of the above."

Excited, she glanced around. "So where is Cade?"

"Over by the waterfall."

A buff blonde, wearing only a Speedo, stood next to the cascading water. His wide, overdeveloped shoulders would look silly in a suit or tuxedo, but that didn't seem to bother the bevy of beauties hanging on his every word. Cynthia gulped.

Immediately, she felt guilty. She knew better than to judge a man by his appearance. That's all anyone had ever done with her. Still… "The blonde?"

"I'm not sure who that is." Henry led her to the other side of the waterfall. A man with wet, dark hair slicked back from his high forehead stood alone. A pineapple cup hid his face. "That's Cade Armstrong Waters."

He was tall. Over six feet. He wore a white T-shirt and green-and-blue plaid swim trunks. He didn't have the other man's muscles, but Cade looked solid and strong.

He lowered the pineapple, and Cynthia breathed a sigh of relief. Cade was good-looking in a geekish sort of way. His small wire-rimmed glasses made him look smart, like a professor. Or a husband. And a father.

He was not a man she would lose herself in. Thank goodness. Cynthia wanted to be a better parent than either of hers had been. Her children would always know they were loved.

On second glance she realized he really wasn't a geek at all. His hair was too long to call him clean-cut and the angles of his face made him look rugged, more than a little dangerous. She swallowed. Hard.

"Like what you see?" Henry asked.

All she could do was nod. That scared her a little. Cynthia remembered Cade came with all those other Armstrongs, and she didn't feel as bad.

Henry laughed. ''Better than Travis?''

''Maybe.'' She forced the word from her dry mouth and adjusted the hibiscus in her hair. ''Let's go. I'm ready for Cade to fall in love with me.''

Cade Waters stirred his drink with the multicolored paper umbrella. He was getting another headache and wanted to call it a night. Nothing about this party interested him. Not the gourmet food, the open bar or the women. Okay, he didn't mind the sarongs or the bikinis, but these women usually wore a lot more clothing and coordinating accessories. Not to mention a pound or two of makeup so they could look ''natural.''

This wasn't his scene. It had been once, a long time ago, but never again. He was a different person now. Money—Armstrong money—had not only destroyed his parents' marriage, but had also ruined Cade's chance for happiness.

Yet here he was.

Cade glanced at the pool on the other side of the waterfall. He'd already swum more laps than he could count which explained why he was so thirsty and hungry, but he preferred being in the water to air-kissing and socializing with people he didn't like, much less respect.

For years, he'd declined Henry's party invitations, much to the dismay of his cousins who loved partying with the generous billionaire. Cade had struggled to move beyond being just another one of the Armstrong cousins. People expected Armstrongs to succeed, and Cade would. He would succeed on his own terms without the help of the Armstrong name or money.

Unfortunately this year he wasn't in a position to say no to Henry Davenport. Call it blackmail, call it desperation. Henry had waved a sizeable donation to Cade's Smiling Moon Foundation with one stipulation—Cade had to attend the birthday party. If he came, did not solicit any of the other guests for donations and stayed until the end of the festivities, Henry would give him a check for one hundred thousand dollars.

Cade had had no choice but to attend. His foundation needed the money. Running a nonprofit agency was more difficult and more expensive than he had imagined. He'd been struggling to make ends meet and if he wasn't careful Smiling Moon might become Frowning Moon and bankrupt if he didn't get a couple of big donors like Henry Davenport.

His parents wanted him to walk away from the foundation and start over with a new venture. Or better yet, return to law. But Cade couldn't. He wouldn't do what his many times divorced parents did when things got tough—leave. He wasn't like that. He wasn't like them. Whether they knew or cared, the kids helped by Smiling Moon would have one adult who didn't abandon them. He would stick it out until the end. And if he had any say in the matter, there wouldn't be an end.

Cade was willing to do anything to keep the foundation going and make it a success even if that meant spending a weekend with a bunch of social climbing, money-burning, socially irresponsible partygoers, a few of whom he was related to on his mother's side. He would overlook Henry's obscene display of wealth. Cade almost passed on taking one of the expensively filled goodie bags each guest received until he realized he could auction it off at his summer fundraising dinner. Provided they survived until the summer. But the designer backpack containing a handheld GPS locator, Swiss Army knife, a dive watch and oyster shells containing pearl earrings or cufflinks depending on a guest's gender would bring a good price.

Henry approached with a wide grin. ''Having fun?''

Cade chose his words carefully. Henry had enough money to make a real difference to the foundation. And if the billionaire birthday boy decided to become a full-fledged patron... Cade smiled at the thought, his first smile in the past forty-eight hours. Or was that forty-eight days? ''It's been...interesting.''

''Happy to hear it.'' Henry motioned to an attractive blonde. ''There's someone I want you to meet.''

Not another one of Henry's women. Cade sipped his rum and coconut concoction and grimaced at the sweet aftertaste. Give him a shot of whiskey or a beer. Can or bottle. Not a froufrou umbrella drink served in a hollowed out pineapple.

''This is Cynthia Sterling, a close friend of mine. Cynthia this is Cade Arm—''

''Cade Waters.'' He glanced over his pineapple at Henry's latest ''friend.'' Cade knew what to expect and he wasn't disappointed. Perfectly cut, dyed and styled blond hair fell past her bare shoulders in gentle waves. Flawless ivory skin, made so by the skilled hand applying her makeup and/or the numerous spa treatments—wraps, peels, facials—she no doubt received regularly, glowed beneath the ballroom lighting. Generous, full lips painted red and able to pout on cue. A deep maroon sarong gave a tantalizing glimpse of the curves underneath and begged to be removed. Cade summed her up in three words—a total nightmare. ''Nice to meet you.''

She extended her arm and batted her eyes. The hazel-green color with gold flecks looked natural, but could be a high-tech pair of contact lenses. "The pleasure's all mine."

The words flowed from her collagen-injected lips like honey. Warm, slow, seductive. Cade managed not to laugh. He'd known too many women like Cynthia Sterling. Trophy-wife wannabes. Gold diggers. Nothing beneath the perfect outer package. His cousins had married and divorced women like her. Hell, some of his Armstrong cousins *were* this type of woman.

But Cynthia Sterling was as far from Cade's type as they came. He knew what he wanted in a woman. Exactly what he wanted. Exactly who he wanted.

Maggie.

But she'll never be yours, a little voice mocked him. *You screwed up.* Cade took another sip of his drink.

"I'll leave you two to get acquainted," Henry said.

Before Cade could say a word, like no, Henry disappeared into the crowded ballroom. Just when Cade thought the party couldn't get any worse...

"So," Cynthia said. "Have you known Henry long?"

Maybe if Cade didn't answer she would go away. He didn't want to be rude, but he wanted to be left alone. Thinking about his ex-fiancée always put him in a rotten mood. He pressed his lips together.

"Henry and I go way back."

A day? A week? Knowing Henry she met him last night. "How long have you been dating?"

"What? Us?" Her laugh, deeper and richer than he expected, surprised him. At least she didn't have an annoying high-pitched squeal. Though that would be the perfect finishing touch for her. Cynthia tilted her chin. "We're just friends. I know better than to date Henry Davenport."

So she was smarter than she looked. Cade had to give

her points for that. He stirred what remained of his drink with the umbrella-on-a-tropical-fruit-skewered-stick.

''What about you?'' she asked.

''I know better than to date Henry, too.''

The smile disappeared from her face and her eyes clouded. ''You're gay? I'm going to kill Henry.'' Before Cade could speak, she continued on. ''That's okay. I mean it's great you're gay. All the good ones seem to be,'' she muttered. ''One of life's ironies. I'm sure you have to beat the men off with a stick or a larger umbrella.''

He lowered his pineapple glass. Of course she had no sense of humor. What had he expected? ''I'm not gay.''

She furrowed her perfectly arched brows. ''But you said—''

''I was making a joke.''

It took a couple of seconds, and the smile returned to her face. ''Oh, I get it now.''

Okay, so she wasn't that smart after all. Henry must see something else in her. Her pretty face, intriguing eyes, incredible body?

Forget about her. Cade was only here to pick up the donation. Once he had Henry's check in hand, Cade was on the next plane home. He glanced into his pineapple. It was empty. ''I need another drink. Want one?''

''Please.'' She smiled, a dazzling smile she'd probably spent hours perfecting in front of a mirror. ''And could you get me one with a pink parasol and a cherry?''

A pink parasol and a cherry? She was the worst possible combination—high-maintenance and high society. Cade held back a sigh. ''I'll do what I can.''

Happy Birthday to me.

Henry Davenport hummed the tune. The party was an

overwhelming success and was only going to get better. Time for two guests to partake in his "adventure." He climbed on stage and the band stopped playing. "Line up for your chance at the adventure of a lifetime," he announced to the crowd.

Tropically and scantily clad, hard-bodied waiters and waitresses passed out drinks to guests who stood in line. No one knew what was in store for the lucky participants. No one cared. People's willingness to participate in his adventures was the only birthday present Henry wanted. Besides, everyonc knew they'd get a nice reward from him when they finished. The more difficult the adventure, the bigger the reward. This year's would be a doozy.

Henry cupped a pair of dice in his hands. This adventure would be his finest triumph. Until next year.

Guests waited for their chance to walk on stage and roll the dice. Cynthia Sterling's turn arrived. She made her way up with a sensual sway of her hips. She was attractive, stunning really, with beautiful hair she had colored every three weeks to give it a natural blond look, and a figure any *Sports Illustrated* model would die for. A brilliant smile lit up her face. Things must be going well with Cade.

Good for her.

Cynthia would never be called sweet or innocent or nice. Truth be told, she was a pain in the butt. But he loved her like a sister and underneath all her makeup, designer clothes and pouty facade lay a good heart.

She was the quintessential poor little rich girl. Her parents were so in love, they barely noticed they'd had a child and she'd grown into a woman. Cynthia deserved to be happy, deserved to be loved. Henry still couldn't believe her parents hadn't remembered her birthday last year. She had shrugged it off. The same way she shrugged off holidays spent alone.

He almost believed she only cared about marrying well, but he'd seen a longing in her eyes the first time she held Noelle. He heard the envy in Cynthia's voice when commenting how perfect Laurel and Brett were together and how lucky they were to have found each other. Cynthia claimed she had no luck finding her Mr. Right. Henry knew she was trying too hard. She was only twenty-six and in a rush to get to the altar. He didn't want her to settle for less than she deserved.

But Cynthia's luck with men was about to change....

She stepped up to the platform and kissed his cheek. "Happy Birthday, Henry."

"Thank you, darling." With a sleight of hand learned from a Reno magician last year, Henry gave her a special pair of dice, different ones than the others had used. "Good luck."

She rubbed the dice between her hands and rolled. Double sixes. High rollers participated in the adventure. One man and one woman. A momentary deer-in-the-headlights expression flashed across her features.

"Don't worry," Henry assured her. "You'll do fine."

Her gaze met his. "I'd better or you'll be the one worrying." Her voice was low, but filled with a threat. He expected no less from her.

Cynthia wasn't meek and mild. She went after what she wanted. The next two weeks weren't going to be easy for her, but they would be good for her. Henry wanted her to be happy. His job was to show Cynthia what she wanted—no, *needed.* And he'd finally figured out the right man for her.

Cade Waters stepped onstage and took the dice. He wasn't thrilled to be here, but he would get over it and come to appreciate what Henry had planned not only for Cade's foundation, but his heart, too.

Cade rolled. Double sixes. He grimaced. Cynthia's full lips broke into a wide smile.

Other guests needed to roll, but Henry couldn't wait for the adventure to begin. This was going to be so much fun. He rubbed his palms together.

The way the adventure would take advantage of Cade's strengths had been a stroke of luck. Henry knew fate had been helping him out. By the time the pair returned from the island adventure, Cynthia would see Cade Waters as her knight in shining khaki, the Indiana Jones of the new millennium, the man of her dreams. Henry tried not to grin too widely. But he had to smile. Life was too good not to have a smile on his face.

Before giving the next guest the dice, Henry discreetly switched them back to the original pair. Once everyone had rolled, he stood at a microphone. "We have our winners. Cynthia Sterling and Cade Armstrong Waters."

The other guests cheered.

"This year, I'm paying homage to the pop-culture phenomena television show *Survivor.* Cade and Cynthia will spend two weeks on a deserted island together."

"Two weeks?" Cade's jaw hardened. "I have responsibilities."

"You'll have time to make arrangements for your absence," Henry said. "You also have the option of paying a penalty fee and not going on the adventure if you choose."

The penalty fee consisted of a ten thousand dollar donation to one of Henry's favorite charities. So far, no one had opted out of an adventure. Along with paying the penalty, one could never attend another one of his birthday parties. He knew Cade was a lawyer and the penalty fee would never stand up in a court of law. But Cade was also counting on a donation to his foundation. Offending the host wouldn't be in his best interest.

Blackmail?

Perhaps, but Henry was only doing what needed to be done. The Smiling Moon Foundation would get a hefty chunk of change no matter how the adventure turned out for Cynthia and Cade. Henry's soft spot for kids had intensified since Noelle's birth.

"I'm in," Cade said with the bravado Henry expected.

"Me, too," Cynthia added.

Of course she was. Two weeks alone with Cade was a dream come true for her. Knowing Cynthia, she was already planning their wedding. The Plaza? The Rainbow Room? And her honeymoon. St. Barts? Turks and Caicos?

"Great." Henry handed them each a backpack. "Pack your toiletries and clothes in these. The rest of the items will be provided when we reach our location."

Holding on to the backpack, Cynthia peered inside. "You want me to pack for two weeks with only this?"

"You don't need much except a swimsuit." At her frown, Henry winked. "Smile, darling. Frowning will give you wrinkles."

She narrowed her eyes. He'd better not push it.

"What about time to make arrangements?" Cade asked. "Two weeks is a long—"

"It's a long trip to our destination," Henry explained. "You'll have time to make calls and get to know each other."

Cade tensed. "Great."

Cynthia's eyes sparkled. "I can't wait."

Neither could Henry.

Chapter Two

Cynthia lounged in a chaise on the deck of Henry's yacht. As she sipped Cristal from a Baccarat flute, the bubbles tickled her nose. She set the glass on a table, and a steward dressed in a white shirt and matching shorts refilled her glass.

This was the life.

Ever since stepping aboard Henry's floating palace last night, she'd been pampered and spoiled by his attentive staff. Who needed a genie in a bottle with Henry around? If her time on the island were anything like the past fourteen hours, she would be living a dream. Too bad Cade wanted no part of it.

She raised her sunglasses and stared at him. He'd barely spoken to her. Not a good sign. She wanted to be noticed, not ignored. "You didn't tell me he was a workaholic."

Henry adjusted his small pillow. "Cade is committed."

"Committed or obsessed?" Cynthia asked. "I don't think he slept last night."

"He's dedicated to his work."

She had to admit his dedication appealed to her. Her father had neglected the family business in order to spend time with her mother until they ended up penniless and homeless when she was twelve. Those four months had been a living hell. It was the only time she had heard her parents argue. Thank goodness her grandfather had come to their rescue once he figured her father had learned his lesson.

But Cynthia hadn't forgotten the uncertainty, the insecurity, the fear. She vowed never to be poor again and planned to marry well so money would never be an issue.

Which brought her back to Cade. He was an Armstrong so he had money. Lots of it. But he also had a job. What a novel idea. She'd never had a job. Nor had Henry. She wondered why Cade had one. "What does he do?"

"He has a law degree." Henry bit into a slice of mango.

Cade must be one of the Armstrong family's personal counsel. Corporate, perhaps? No matter, he must make a bundle or he would simply live off his inheritance.

A lawyer.

Maybe Cade wanted to go into politics like a few of his more visible cousins. Cynthia didn't consider herself political, but she took her right to vote seriously. Politics could be interesting if Cade leaned in that direction. She could be the wife of a governor, a senator, the president.

First Lady.

All that attention and adoration. People would love her. Delight shivered through Cynthia. She would like to be First Lady. She would be a good First Lady. No, a great one. She would be perfect to set fashion and hair trends.

She'd usher in a style and sophistication level not seen since the Kennedy era.

Of course that would be years away. Cade was much too young to be elected president but not too young for Congress.

"So Cade is a lawyer." And the future leader of this great nation. Cynthia lowered her sunglasses. She would stand by his side and together they would go down in the history books. The country would love her. The world would love her. Most importantly, Cade would love her.

Henry dabbed his mouth with a napkin. "Let Cade tell you what he does."

"I want him to tell me a lot of things."

Henry laughed. "You'll have plenty of time for that."

"Not if Cade spends the entire time working."

"No phones, Palm Pilots or laptops allowed on the island."

"Good. Very good." She settled back in her lounge chair. "I only wish Cade would stop working now and join us. How is he going to fall in love with me without knowing me?"

"Patience, darling." Henry held up his glass, and the steward added more champagne. "Once you get to the island, Cade is all yours."

"All mine."

Henry nodded. "In two weeks time, the two of you will be inseparable."

That sounded good to her. She wanted Cade to fall head over heels in love with her. Two weeks together would allow that to happen. By the time they left the island he wouldn't want her out of his sight. "Cynthia Armstrong."

"Cynthia Waters," Henry corrected.

A warm feeling settled around her heart. "It still has a nice ring to it."

"That it does, darling." Henry raised his glass. "That it does."

After a long morning spent working inside, Cade stepped on deck, squinted in the bright sunlight and walked to the rail. As the ship cut a path through the waves, a refreshing breeze blew. The scent of saltwater permeated the air. A sea of blue stretched all the way to the horizon.

He allowed himself a moment to enjoy the peacefulness and the beauty. A minute passed. Then another.

Okay, long enough. Cade wasn't here for R&R. He was here because of a donor's whim. No way could he enjoy himself.

His forehead throbbed. He didn't have two weeks to waste out in the middle of the Pacific. Vacations were a luxury. One he could live without. He had too many responsibilities, commitments, work. Sure, he took a day off here and there and even attended his sister's impromptu wedding in Lake Tahoe on Valentine's Day. But he hadn't had a real vacation in over three years. Or was it five? He couldn't remember.

But this wasn't a vacation. This was for the survival of Smiling Moon and all the kids the foundation helped.

And what about his family? They needed him, too. His dad acted happy enough with wife number six, but Cade's mother was between marriages again and his sister, Kelsey, was a newlywed. His brother-in-law, Will, seemed like a good guy, but what if a problem arose and Cade was unable to help?

The throbbing turned into a full-blown headache. He massaged his temples.

Henry joined him at the railing. ''Did you finish making your arrangements?''

Cade nodded.

''I know this is more than you agreed to.''

He nodded again. Cade didn't trust what words might come out of his mouth. Damn, he hated the walking-on-eggshells-kissing-up part of donor wooing.

''Are you going to stay for the entire two weeks?''

Cade nearly laughed. ''Do I have a choice?''

Henry's carefree smile contradicted the slyness in his eyes. ''You always have a choice.''

Not always. ''I finish what I start.'' Cade would make it to the end of the adventure. He'd only walked away from one thing in his life. And he'd lived to regret it.

''Good, because if you do I'll increase my donation...significantly.''

Leave it to Henry to dangle the right carrot. ''What about—''

''Cynthia?''

Cade nodded. ''She doesn't look like the outdoors type.''

''There's more to her than meets the eye,'' Henry said. ''I hope you give her a chance.''

''We won't have a problem.'' As long as she stays out of the way. Cade could survive whatever Henry threw at him. Surviving Cynthia Sterling, however, was another story.

The more Cade saw of her, the more he realized his first impression had been correct. She was the polar opposite of Maggie, and the kind of woman Cade avoided like the plague.

He realized Cynthia's last name fit her better than her first name. She was Sterling—sterling silver to be exact. She needed to be taken care of, polished and buffed or she would tarnish. He hoped she could do it herself for the next two weeks because he didn't have the time.

"I forgot one thing." Henry's gaze met his. "Cynthia has to make it to the end with you or you won't get *any* donation."

"What?"

"Both you and Cynthia have to remain on the island for two weeks. Or you lose. Everything."

Cade's heart plummeted to his feet. The socialite wouldn't last two hours, let alone two weeks. "That's not fair."

Henry shrugged.

"She'll never make it."

"You'll have to see that she does."

"That's—"

"My prerogative," Henry interrupted. "My birthday, my adventure, my rules."

Your money.

Cade had no options. What could he do? Sue Henry for the original donation? That wasn't going to happen because he only had an oral agreement. They hadn't shook on it, either. This wasn't looking good. Until Cade got an idea. "Fine, we'll both make it to the end, but I not only want a significant donation, I want you to agree to become a patron of the Smiling Moon foundation and make an annual pledge. And I want it all in writing before I step foot off this ship."

Henry drew his brows together. "Five."

"Five what?"

"Five million a year. And I will put it in writing. Though we won't be able to have it notarized." Henry looked at Cade. "Will that do?"

He stood speechless and swallowed around a lump the size of Fort Knox lodged in his throat. "That'll do."

Cade spoke calmly, more rationally than he thought possible, given the way he fought not to pump his fists, jump up and down and yell. Hell, he wanted to hug Henry.

Five million dollars a year exceeded Cade's wildest dreams, every expectation he'd had. His foundation operated on a shoestring budget thanks to his Uncle Alan curtailing Cade's access to his trust fund so he couldn't give all his money away. But the foundation had survived. And with Henry's donation, would thrive. The taste of sweet success filled Cade.

"Just remember Cynthia has to be there at the end."

Nothing, especially a pampered socialite, would keep the foundation from receiving the bigger donation. "She will be."

Cade was going to make sure of it.

Time was running out for Cade. The stakes for winning the adventure had gone way up. He had to find Sterling and make plans while they had the chance.

As Henry prepared for their arrival at the island down in his cabin, Cade made his way to the stern. She had to be here somewhere. Sunlight gleamed off the pool water, but she wasn't there. All the lounge chairs were empty. She couldn't have fallen overboard. He didn't have that kind of luck.

He found her lying under the protective shade of a giant umbrella. No doubt she wanted to keep her fair skin away from the tropical sun. Or maybe she was just lounging around. He gritted his teeth.

An omen of things to come? Cade hoped not, but he wouldn't be surprised if she expected him to do all the work. And that might not be so bad. He had experience backpacking in wilderness areas and knew what needed to be done. She didn't. It might be easier this way. Too bad he couldn't vote her off the island, but he knew Henry wouldn't go for that suggestion.

Cade walked toward her. She wore a white cap-sleeve blouse that buttoned up the front and pink Capri pants with a pair of the most uncomfortable looking sandals he'd ever seen. No wonder she was lying down. Those shoes with the narrow straps and high heels must be murder on the feet.

She wore sunglasses even in the shade. She probably wore a silky eye mask when she slept, too. He didn't know if she was asleep or awake now, but he didn't care. They needed to talk without Henry around.

"Are you awake?" Cade wasn't sure what their upcoming adventure entailed, but the key to survival and success was preparation. He didn't expect much from Sterling, but a little help was better than nothing. And for better or worse, they were in this together.

No answer.

He nudged the chaise with his foot. "Sterling?"

No movement.

"You need to wake up." He touched her knee. "Now."

Raising her hands above her head, she stretched slowly like a cat waking from an afternoon nap. Cade watched with a mixture of fascination and horror. He felt like a peeping Tom yet he couldn't look away as the bottom of her shirt rose. Above her pants, above her belly button, above the bottom of her rib cage. Sweat dripped down his back.

Damn, the sun was hot in the tropics.

He brushed his hand through his hair and adjusted his glasses on the bridge of his nose.

She sat up. "Hello, Cade."

Her voice sounded deeper, almost husky. Especially

when she said his name. Cade wondered why he noticed the difference. He also wondered why he missed the sight of her bare midriff.

No matter. They had more important issues to worry about. ‘‘We need to talk.’’

She scooted over and patted the small space next to her. ‘‘Why don’t you join me?’’

The collar of his T-shirt seemed to tighten. ‘‘I’ll stand.’’

She removed her sunglasses. ‘‘What did you have on your mind?’’

You. ‘‘Henry’s adventure.’’

Her smile widened. ‘‘It’s going to be fun.’’

‘‘Fun?’’ Cade stared into her eyes. She had nice eyes. And he really liked all those little gold flecks.

‘‘Yes, fun,’’ she said. ‘‘What more could you ask for? Two whole weeks on a deserted island. Just the two of us for fourteen days.’’

‘‘Fourteen days,’’ he echoed.

She nodded with an intriguing—suggestive?—glint in her eyes. ‘‘Fourteen days and nights.’’

The nights might turn out to be the best part. He smiled.

What the hell am I doing? Cade looked away. The sun was getting to him. He’d have to drink more water. Or wear a hat. ‘‘Have you ever watched *Survivor?*’’

‘‘Once or twice at a party, but I didn’t pay too much attention. The people were so dirty and starving.’’ She wrinkled her nose. ‘‘How much fun is that?’’

‘‘Exactly.’’ This wasn’t going to be as bad as he thought. At least she knew what they were up against. ‘‘I don’t know what Henry has in mind, but I’m assuming it will be similar to the show. He’ll stick us on a deserted island and make us compete against each other for rewards.’’

''Henry would never pit us against each other.'' Confidence laced each of her words. ''There's no way that would happen.''

''Maybe not, but, we need to be prepared. Come on.''

Cade walked toward the lounge. The click of her ridiculous heels on the wooden deck told him she was following.

''Where are we going?'' she asked.

''To raid the galley. We have to be ready for whatever Henry throws at us such as not giving us any rations.'' At her blank stare, Cade clarified it. ''Food. He might not give us any food.''

She pursed her lips. ''Henry wouldn't do that to us.''

Cade wished he had her confidence. ''What if he does?''

''He won't.''

She had so much trust in her friendship with Henry. Cade couldn't afford such blind loyalty again. He headed down the stairs to the galley. Fortunately none of the crew milled about. ''Without food we'll have to eat bugs and worms and snakes and a whole lot of other nasty stuff.''

''Henry will give us food.'' Certainty filled her voice. ''I've never swatted a fly. How could he expect me to eat one?''

Cade didn't have time to change her mind. ''Fine, we'll have food, but let's bring a few extra things to eat.''

''You mean snacks?''

''Snacks, food, whatever we can fit in our backpacks.''

''My backpack's full.''

''You'll have to make room.'' He struggled to keep his voice low and calm. Losing his temper would solve nothing and only bring attention to their whereabouts. ''We don't have much time. I can do this on my own, but I'd rather we did it together. Are you in, Sterling?''

She grinned. "I'm in, Armstrong."

He hated that name, hated everything associated with it. "It's Waters."

"I'm sorry."

He handed her a plastic bag and kept one for himself. "You stand guard first, while I go in. Then we switch. Got it?"

She nodded. "We're going to make a good team, Cade."

He doubted that, but as long as they survived until the end he didn't care. "Let me know if someone is coming."

"Will it work if I whistle?" She put her lips together and blew. It looked as if she was waiting for a kiss.

"A whistle is—" he dragged his eyes away from her puckered lips "—fine."

More than fine coming from her lips, but he wasn't going there. Not today, tomorrow or any time in the next two weeks.

"The two weeks are going to fly by," Henry said to her and Cade as they rode to shore in a small boat. He motioned to the cove in front of them. "What do you think of your new home?"

Cynthia stared at the picture postcard island paradise. A movie set couldn't have captured the lagoon with clear blue water, towering palm trees and a crescent of sparkling white sand any more perfectly. "It's breathtaking."

"Lucky us," Cade said. "Our own *Gilligan's Island.*"

"I get to be Ginger," Cynthia said.

The boat stopped twenty-five feet from shore. Crew members unloaded two wooden crates and carried them to shore. As soon as they reached the beach, music played. Drums, chanting, an eerie flutelike instrument.

Cynthia looked around for the mysterious source. She

noticed a boom box sitting near Henry's feet and immediately felt better. For a minute she thought they were arriving at *Fantasy Island.* At least that would explain why Henry wore an all white suit like Mr. Roarke.

Henry rose. "Your adventure begins now. For the next two weeks, you will live on this island. There's a radio for emergencies, but otherwise you are on your own. Basic provisions have been provided. The rest you will need to find, make or win. I'll stop by on a regular basis to check up on you and play a few games."

"What kind of games?" Cynthia asked.

"Games to challenge your ability to survive on the island," Henry explained. "And you win prizes by playing."

Cynthia clapped. "I love prizes."

"That's the spirit." He grinned. "Ready to go ashore?"

Cade removed his shoes, slung his backpack over his shoulder and hopped out of the boat. As he waded to shore, he passed the crewmen on their way back.

"Go on," Henry urged.

"I'll get wet." The beach wasn't far, but her stomach knotted and she thought she might be sick at the idea of getting in the water. "I don't want to get wet."

"The water's nice and warm," Cade yelled.

"No." Fear paralyzed her. She'd been caught in a riptide when she was eight. Since then she hadn't been in the water except for sitting in a bathtub or a Jacuzzi. No one noticed she never swam. "The saltwater will ruin my clothes."

"Come on, Sterling."

Ever since their successful raids on the galley, Cade had called her Sterling. Cynthia worried he might have forgotten her first name. At this point her name didn't matter, but she would ask Henry a million questions if it kept her out of the water. "Why does Cade keep calling me by my last name?"

"Men often call each other by their last names."

She put her hands on her hips. "Do I look like a man?"

Henry gave her the once-over. "Not in the slightest."

"Thank you."

"Get in the water, Cynthia," Henry said.

So much for stalling. Think, think… "Have him carry me to shore," she whispered.

"Brilliant idea. One I should have thought of." Henry beamed. "Cade, carry her to shore."

"What?" he asked.

"Carry Cynthia to shore," Henry suggested. "That's what a gentleman would do."

Cade mumbled something about not being a gentleman, but Cynthia couldn't hear his exact words. Still he dropped his backpack on the beach and waded back to the boat.

"Thanks," she mouthed to Henry.

"I've done my part. The rest is up to you."

By the time Cade reached the boat, he'd drawn his lips into a thin line. "The water isn't deep."

Cynthia had learned deep was a relative term. She forced a smile and batted her eyelashes. "Please?"

A beat passed. He nodded once.

"Thanks." This time her smile was genuine. Not only had she maneuvered her way out of getting in the water, she was going to end up in Cade's arms. It would be like the scene in *Gone with the Wind* when Rhett carried Scarlett up the stairs. Yes, a brilliant idea. Her first of many during the next fourteen days.

As Cade grabbed her backpack, she rose. Anticipation filled her. His hands clasped around her waist. A bevy of butterflies attacked her stomach. She waited for him to lift her into his arms. He slung her over his left shoulder like a Prada bag instead.

Staring at the water, she pushed herself up his back. ''What—''

''You're not as light as you look.'' His hand clamped on the back of her thigh. ''Stop wiggling or I'm going to drop you.''

She didn't move a muscle; she didn't blink. She couldn't. The heat from his hands radiated through the fabric of her capris. Hot. Burning. Okay, so this wasn't the romantic scene she'd envisioned, but talk about a turn-on.

This was not a good thing. In fact, it was a very bad thing. She wanted to feel comfortable with Cade, chummy and cuddly like she had with Travis. Not all hot and bothered wondering if Cade would move his hand up a couple more inches. The goal was for him to get lost in her, not the other way around. She wasn't going to repeat her parents' mistake.

He dropped her unceremoniously on the sand. ''Next time, you're getting wet.''

No next time. No water. No touching.

Cade handed her the backpack. ''Thanks,'' she said.

No ''you're welcome'' or ''not a problem.'' Simply nothing. She didn't understand. Most men wanted her gratitude.

The horn from the boat sliced through the silence. Henry waved. ''I'll be back tomorrow. Have fun tonight.''

Cynthia blew him a kiss and waved. She turned and faced a tense-looking Cade. Maybe he was jealous of Henry. She didn't want to start out on the wrong foot.

Not when she wanted Cade to like her. ''Want a kiss, too?''

''Only if it's chocolate.''

Now he was talking. She moistened her lips. ''Those are my second favorite kind.''

Chapter Three

What had he done to deserve Sterling?

They were on an island and she didn't want to get wet. She was more pampered than a Persian show cat. Forget about being here at the end of the two weeks. She'd be lucky to survive tonight.

Cade watched her pick up her backpack, ease the strap onto her shoulder and straighten it. No doubt years of cruising malls and boutiques with shopping bags and a large purse had trained her well. Only her shopping expertise was worthless here. So were those high-heeled sandals. The thin straps made her ankles look so delicate. The heels accentuated her toned calves. At least they were good for something. They weren't designed for walking or comfort or anything remotely practical. "You might want to take off your shoes," he suggested.

"The sand is hot." She took a wobbly step in the hourglass-fine sand. And another. It was like watching a train wreck.

One more step and her ankle gave way. She stumbled

and plopped onto the sand with a delicate exclamation. A heap of legs, arms and backpack. She brushed the sand from her hands with a bit of impatience.

He walked toward her. ''You okay?''

''Yes.'' Frustration laced her words. As she undid the strap circling her thin ankle, she fumbled with the catches. Finally she removed the sandals. ''I should have listened to you.''

''The sand *is* hot.'' Cade wanted to be charitable if not nice. No matter what he might think of Sterling, he was going to be the picture of restraint and politeness. That was the only way they would survive this ordeal together. Fourteen days with her? The thought made him grit his teeth. ''Want a hand?''

''Please.''

He extended his arm, and his hand engulfed hers. Her skin felt soft and smooth against his. Warm, too. Her hand was so small, but she was no wispy flower about to wilt in the sun. He'd found that out when he carried her to shore. She was soft, but well toned. No doubt she worked out.

As Cade pulled Sterling to her feet, he caught a whiff of her perfume. No light and airy fragrance for her, either. Her scent was exotic, yet subtle. The kind of perfume that left an imprint and made him want another smell. But that wasn't an option. She wasn't one, either.

He let go of her hand. ''I hope you brought other shoes.''

''Of course, I did. They are the most beautiful pair of Manolo…'' Her smile disappeared. ''They have heels, too. No matter, I'll simply buy another pair.''

Cade glanced around. Palm trees, sand, shrubbery. Not a shoe store in sight. ''Where?''

''At the resort.''

"What resort?"

She stared at him as if he'd asked the stupidest question in the world. "The one we're staying at for our adventure."

Uh-oh. Cade looked out to sea. A small dot sailed toward the horizon. He had one word for Henry. *Chicken.* Cade actually had several more, but he'd joined the kids at Smiling Moon's challenge to stop swearing. Until now, he'd forgotten, but he needed to make an effort for the kids' sake.

"What's wrong?" Sterling asked.

Might as well tell her the truth. She'd figure it out for herself soon enough. "We're on a deserted island, Sterling. There is no resort."

"There has to be a resort."

"Sorry." He didn't know what else to say.

"If there's no resort, where will we sleep?" She tilted her chin with an inquisitive look in her eyes. "A hotel?"

He dug the toe of his shoe into the sand. "Right here."

Her forehead creased, but she still didn't seem to get it.

"Out here on the beach," he added. "Or maybe back by the trees. We'll have to scout out a good campsite. Among the trees would be the best."

Her eyes widened. "You mean we'll sleep outside like...camping in a t-tent?"

He nodded. "A tent would be a luxury. Remember this is a survival adventure. Henry wants us to use survival skills."

"Put me in a motel with poly-cotton blend sheets and no room service and I'll show you survival skills. This...this is inhumane." Her words held an edge of panic. She glanced around. "Where are the...facilities?"

"Do you mean bathrooms?"

She nodded.

"Wherever you want them to be."

Her mouth gaped open. "You mean…in the wild?"

The horror in her voice almost made Cade feel sorry for her. "This isn't exactly the wild, but the answer is yes."

She pursed her lips. Yes, she had the perfect pout down pat. He was surprised she didn't stomp her feet or toss her shoes to the ground. No doubt that's what she would do next.

"How could Henry do this to us? To me?" Her eyes glistened and Cade thought she might cry. "Henry's supposed to be my friend. He's like a brother to me."

Cade took a step toward her and stopped. He didn't know what to do. Hug her? He didn't want to give her the wrong idea. She wasn't his friend. She was his responsibility for the next two weeks. Nothing more, nothing less.

"Henry said this would be a fun adventure. I'm usually up for anything, but this…" She blinked. "What was he thinking? Henry knows I've never been camping."

Cade understood Sterling's frustration. He didn't want to be here any more than she did, but he could imagine this was a lot worse for her than him. She probably didn't use public restrooms or know what a latrine was. "It'll be okay."

"No, it won't." Her gaze, full of fear, locked on Cade. "I don't want to die in the wild."

"No one is going to die." Like her or not, he would have to cut her some slack. He squeezed her hand. "I've spent lots of time outdoors. Hiking, backpacking, climbing, camping."

"So you know what to do?"

‘‘I know what to do,’’ he assured her. ‘‘I’ll—we’ll be fine.’’

Her brilliant smile made him feel like her hero. A superhero to Henry’s treacherous villain? No, Cade wouldn’t go that far, but he enjoyed spending time outdoors and knew what he was doing. He’d chaperoned a group of kids backpacking on the Pacific Coast Trail and another group on a climb up Mount Shasta. If he could handle a bunch of kids from broken homes with chips on their shoulders the size of Asia, he could manage Sterling. Sure she didn’t come from a broken home and her chip was diamond, but the principle was the same. He just needed a softer touch.

Soft like her skin.

He was still holding her hand. He let go as if it were a stick of dynamite about to blow. Touching her again seemed like a really bad idea. Almost as bad as agreeing to the adventure. He motioned to the wooden crates. ‘‘Let’s see what’s inside.’’

Cade pried open the lid and removed the contents: toilet paper, cloth napkins, one blanket, a ball of string, a canvas cloth, a plastic tarp, two towels and washcloths, eating and serving utensils, two pots, two mugs, two plates, a plastic bag filled with matches, two rain ponchos, two flashlights and a first aid kit. ‘‘No food.’’

‘‘It’ll be in the other box.’’ Sterling’s voice lacked her earlier confidence.

He opened the second crate and pulled out the contents: a battery-operated radio and microphone, sunscreen, lip balm, a container of rice, another of coffee, a bottle of multivitamins, salt and pepper, two buckets and two canteens. He found a handwritten letter at the bottom of the crate.

To my lucky participants,
Welcome to the Isle of Davenport. I purchased it specifically for your adventure so enjoy all this beautiful island has to offer. The crates contain basic supplies to get you started. The rest is up to you to find, make or win during one of my games. You will face a series of tests and challenges. Whoever wins gets a prize. You'll find a water tank beyond the trees. Enclosed is a map to a fresh water source. I recommend boiling the water before drinking it. I can't think of anything else to write except it does rain so get a shelter built ASAP. Have fun, my friends, and see you tomorrow.
All my best,
H.

Egomaniac. Cade clenched his jaw. "Henry needs to be sent on his own adventure. The bast—uh, bashful guy."

Sterling looked dumbfounded. "He didn't leave us any food except some rice. How much rice can one person eat? White rice isn't food. It doesn't even make a good side dish."

"Don't forget, we brought our own food." Cade didn't want her to worry. Or cry. He opened his pack and pulled out an orange, a bag of crackers, a jar of peanut butter, two cans of tomatoes and three cans of beans. "At least we won't be eating tree bark or other nasty stuff."

He expected a smile; he didn't get one. Uh-oh. The chef had interrupted them so Cade hadn't seen what Sterling had taken from the galley. "You packed food, right?"

"I—I did." She clutched her backpack. "But I was thinking more along the lines of snacks and..."

"And what? Show me what you brought." She looked like a rabbit snared in a trap and guilt surged through him. He hadn't meant to raise his voice, but he was feeling the pressure. Cade took a deep breath. Like it or not, he was going to have to make sure they both got through the next two weeks. "Whatever you packed will be fine."

She pulled a small jar of stuffed olives from a side pocket of her backpack. Olives wouldn't have been his first choice, but it could have been a lot worse.

He smiled. "Good job."

Next she removed a clear bottle from the main compartment.

"What is it?" he asked.

"Gin." Pride filled her eyes. "We can make martinis."

Martinis? Cade's blood pressure soared off the charts. It was all he could do not to lose it. He wasn't sure how, but he managed to keep smiling. Even as he calculated the number of cans of beans she could have packed in the same space. "I would have never thought of that."

"Did you think about dessert?" She pulled three Godiva chocolate bars from the backpack's front pocket. "I can't live without chocolate."

Cade blew out a puff of air. They had all they needed for hangovers and cavities. Not that it mattered since they were going to starve to death. At least they would go in style—drunk and on a sugar high.

She removed a small can of mandarin oranges, four granola bars and a pear. "The pear's not ripe, but I thought that would be better since it would last longer."

Okay, she was redeeming herself for the martinis. "Great."

"And my pièce de résistance…" She removed a small can from the other side pocket.

Excitement rushed through him. "Tuna."

"No, it's caviar. Not Beluga, but it will do."

Cade would have preferred Starkist. A can of Spam would have been more useful than caviar. Oh, well… "Let's put all the food in here."

She frowned. "You're disappointed in me."

Cade grabbed one of the empty crates. "I'm not."

"You are." She fiddled with one of the zippers on her pack. "I can see it in your face."

"You aren't seeing anything on my face."

Her lower lip quivered and she blinked. Once, twice. Oh, hel—heck. She was going to cry.

"You did good, Sterling. You really did."

Her eyes filled with tears.

"Please don't cry."

Too late. Tears streamed down her cheeks.

Damn. He meant darn. He hated tears. Every time the kids at the foundation cried, it tore his heart out. Tears reminded him of his childhood and all the fights between his parents both pre-and post-divorce. He and Kelsey used to take turns crying and comforting. More than once they both ended up in tears.

"I'm sorry," Sterling said.

"You did fine. Great. We're going to have a good breakfast in the morning with the granola bars."

Her tears continued to flow. Cade thought his father and uncle Alan were old-fashioned for carrying monogrammed linen handkerchiefs. Cade wished he had one now. He grabbed a washcloth from the crates and handed the cloth to her. "Here."

She dried the tears. Her makeup was a mess, her eyes red. For the first time since he'd met her she didn't look perfect. She looked vulnerable and scared and he felt like a jerk. "I'm sorry for making you cry."

"I'm sorry for crying and for only bringing snacks."

She sniffled. "Things aren't turning out the way I imagined. I have a tendency to cry if I—I'm out of my element."

She was going to be out of her element for the next two weeks. Fourteen days of tears. *Thanks a lot, Henry.*

Cade would have to keep his voice down. He'd learned to remain calm no matter what the kids did. He never raised his voice unless safety was an issue. He'd treat Sterling like one of the kids. That would do the trick.

Except for one problem. She didn't look like one of the kids. Nor smell like one. Nor... No, he wasn't going there.

"You won't be out of your element long," he explained with the same tone he'd used with Jimmy Richardson, who'd figured out halfway up Mt. Shasta he was scared of heights. "In a few days, you'll feel right at home. Trust me."

"I do trust you, Cade."

Her gaze held his. He saw she trusted him and he couldn't understand why. She didn't know him. Maggie had known everything about him, yet that hadn't been enough. Regret twisted around his heart, and he looked away. "We need to build a shelter."

"I've never built anything before."

"There's always a first time."

"Yes, there is." She straightened her shoulders. "What do I do?"

"Collect as many branches as you can. Bamboo, too." He pointed to a clearing beneath some trees. "Pile stuff there. Whatever you think we can use, add it to the stack."

"I—I can do that."

As long as she kept that attitude, they would be fine.

He reached for the map to the fresh water. "I'll get the water. We don't want to be searching in the dark."

She handed him the two buckets. "Don't get lost."

The seriousness in her eyes contradicted her light-hearted tone. Concern for him or herself? Cade realized out here it was both. He glanced at the map. "It isn't far."

Sterling went to work with an enthusiasm that surprised him. Dragging palm fronds to the clearing, she looked at him. "You'd better get going."

"You'll be fine."

She nodded and Cade's respect for her went up a notch. Perhaps there was more to Sterling than high heels, caviar and champagne. As he made his way to the trail he heard the rustling of tree leaves and branches.

"Oh, no," Sterling cried.

Cade glanced back. "What happened?"

"I chipped a nail." She raised her hand in the air. "You didn't happen to pack a manicure set, did you?"

Maybe he'd spoken too soon. Cade took a breath and exhaled slowly. "No, but I have a Swiss Army knife."

Cynthia wanted to sit down, but she didn't dare. She was afraid if she sat, she wouldn't be able to stand again. Muscles she didn't know she had hurt. The bottoms of her bare feet ached. They'd been working for hours and still weren't finished.

Using her forearm, she wiped the perspiration—no, sweat—from her face. Perspiration didn't begin to describe what working in this scalding temperature was doing to her body. Not to mention all the dirt mixed with the sunscreen. Talk about disgusting. She needed a shower. Make that a bubble bath, followed by a facial and a massage. After that she'd stay in bed at least twenty-four hours to recover from this trauma.

''You okay?'' Cade asked for the umpteenth time.

No, she wasn't okay. Her muscles ached, her hands throbbed and she wanted to crawl into a hole and die. But somehow she forced her lips upward. The small movement hurt. Whoever said it took fewer muscles to smile than frown was wrong. ''I'm fine.''

''Drink lots of water so you don't get dehydrated.''

With a nod that sent her head spinning, she raised a canteen to her already chapped and peeling lips. The water flowed down her throat. She felt better, refreshed. Now if they had air-conditioning…

''You can take a break if you're tired.''

No way would she quit first. Cade hadn't been impressed with her tears, but she'd seen his expression change when she'd jumped into the task he assigned her. Cynthia hadn't expected him to want her to do any work. She only asked to be polite and was shocked when he'd taken her up on the offer. Most men wanted her to sit around looking pretty so this was a new experience and she didn't want to let Cade down. ''We can both rest when we're done.''

Which meant they would never sleep again.

The shelter, Cade called it a ''lean-to,'' still wasn't finished, and so far she'd chipped or broken four nails and had a nasty blister on the index finger of her right hand. Two more weeks of this and she'd be a total wreck. She didn't want to think about what tomorrow would bring. Or the next day. Or the next. Who was she kidding? She wasn't going to make it. She'd be lucky to survive tonight. By the end of today she would be nothing more than a huge aching muscle covered with blisters.

This island might look like a tropical paradise, but

without a day spa, a hair salon, a manicurist and air-conditioning, she was at an extreme disadvantage of getting through the day let alone getting Cade to fall in love with her.

With no electricity she wasn't going to be able to use her blow dryer, hot rollers or curling iron. Talk about bad hair days. She wasn't sure how they would bathe. The thought of being this dirty for two whole weeks nauseated her. Forget about any cuddling or kissing. Romance and dirtiness were incompatible.

This was worse than any episode of *Survivor.* At least those people got to be on television. And a few even looked good without makeup.

Makeup. Her heart tightened.

Forget about it. Foundation melted and ran off her face in this heat and humidity. She might be able to still wear eyeliner and lipstick, but other than that...

It was hopeless. Completely and utterly hopeless.

What was Henry thinking with this ridiculous adventure?

He'd gotten her hopes up only to have them come crashing down like a tree loaded with coconuts. She was going to kill him. Somehow, someday, she would get even.

This was so unfair.

Cynthia heard a noise and glanced up. She'd never seen a man work so hard. Cade had been building their shelter all day. She stared at his back.

Okay, not everything on this island was horrible. She enjoyed watching him sans shirt. A tiny bit of white sneaked out from the waistband of his shorts. Briefs, she realized. Boxers would be more comfortable in this heat. She, herself, couldn't wait to change into her swimsuit, but she didn't want grime covering every inch of her skin.

But she liked seeing Cade's skin gleaming with sweat. She'd never found that attractive until now. He had more muscles than she realized and each one was getting a workout. Nice shoulders, nice back, nice butt, nice legs. Good, she could appreciate Cade without totally obsessing over him. That was something positive on an otherwise negative day.

"Can you hold this for me?" he asked.

Cynthia screwed the cap on her canteen and hurried to his side. "What do you want me to do?"

"Keep these branches together."

She grabbed hold of them. "Like this?"

"Yes, but..."

He placed his hands on top of hers. His hands were rough and dirty, but she didn't care. That surprised her.

"It'll be easier if you hold them like this."

Heat radiated from his hands, his breath, him. He'd removed his glasses and looked more rugged. More handsome. More male. Her pulse picked up speed and her throat went dry. The reaction wasn't from the heat. No, this was strictly due to Cade. And it had to stop. She didn't want him to have this effect on her.

"Do you have it?" he asked.

"Oh, yes." He left her tongue-tied and acting like a freshman with a crush on a senior. She liked the feeling. No, she reminded herself, she did not. She wasn't about to be consumed by any man. That wouldn't be fair to her future children. She squared her shoulders.

"I'm going to tie this to the sides of the lean-to. The canvas cloth will cover the bamboo floor and I'll put the ponchos on top of the palms when we finish the roof to keep us dry during rainstorms."

Cade really knew what he was doing, and a few of the fears she had at being in the wilderness disappeared. No matter what, she was in good hands. He handled being in this foreign environment so well. She could only imagine how he would be in the courtroom or the boardroom. Or the Oval Office.

"Okay." He tied off the string. "I've got it. Thanks."

"Anytime."

His gaze met hers. "You can let go now."

No, she couldn't. She had to figure out how to breathe first. He made her feel naked, exposed. All the things she shouldn't feel with him. She jerked her hands away. "Sorry."

"No need to apologize."

He wasn't laughing at her, but his eyes seemed to be. Her cheeks warmed. She really felt like a teenager. And she hated being one of those. She'd been too thin, too tall, too ugly. She'd looked so much like her father it was frightening. She'd spent years perfecting the way she looked now—almost a carbon copy of her mother. Of course the last person she ever wanted to *behave* like was her mother or her father. Cynthia sighed.

Cade's eyes darkened. "Something wrong?"

"No."

He wiped his hands on his shorts. "So what do you think?"

You're gorgeous. But she suspected that wasn't what he was asking. "About what?"

"The shelter." He pointed to the half-built lean-to. "It might not look like much yet, but it's going to be our home for the next two weeks."

She clasped her hands and placed them over her heart. "Our first home together."

"I hope you don't expect me to carry you over the threshold once it's completed."

"I didn't think lean-tos had thresholds."

"They don't."

The corners of his mouth lifted. Okay, this was much better. She liked his smile, the way his eyes crinkled and softened his face. She wanted soft and fluffy, a teddy bear. He'd been too much of a grizzly up to now. "So how shall we celebrate moving in?"

"Dinner?"

"Too mundane." She wet her lips and wondered if her twelve-hour lipstick would last in this heat. "How about we toast our new abode with martinis at sunset?"

"Don't you need vermouth for a martini?"

"So we'll have gin and olives at sunset. I'm flexible."

Determination flashed in his eyes. "I'm counting on that."

Chapter Four

The cloudless, blue sky from the morning turned a dark and ominous gray by afternoon. Cade carried the last palm frond to the shelter. ''We have to hurry.''

Sterling wiped her mouth with the back of her hand. Her unpainted, unglossed lips were chapped, but Cade liked her mouth better without all the makeup. Her full lips looked more attractive. Natural. Not collagen-injected. Would he be able to tell if they were real or not by kissing her?

Where did that come from? He would not be kissing her. Ever.

''I don't see what the big rush is,'' she said.

''Rain.''

''It rains every afternoon in the Tropics.'' She screwed the cap on her canteen. ''The air's so hot and humid, a rain shower will feel good. Refreshing. When I was in Antigua—''

''The South Pacific is a world away from the Caribbean.'' The front moving in wasn't bringing a refreshing afternoon shower. A downpour or typhoon was more likely. ''It looks like a storm.''

''Oh, no. It won't storm.''

Cade wondered if she had a wireless connection to The Weather Channel, but he didn't have time to argue. Only a patch of blue sky remained. A storm *was* moving in, and they weren't ready. He would have to try a different tact. ''Maybe not, but if we want martinis at sunset, we need to have the lean-to completed, a fire going and all the supplies stored in the crates.''

''Why didn't you just say so?'' She wiped her hands on her no-longer pink pants. ''Tell me what to do.''

''Hand me the fronds I laid out for the roof. Please,'' he added as an afterthought.

''The what?''

''The palm branches.'' Cade took the first one she offered. ''Hold it for me, okay?''

''No problem.''

Not for her. Not when she *was* the problem. His problem.

Okay, she had done more work than he thought she would. She'd dragged branches to the campsite and helped him build the lean-to, but she acted as if they were at Club Med and doing this for fun. This was about their survival, their ability to make it to the end. There was nothing fun about it. He wondered when she would finally get it.

She held out another branch. ''Don't you think it would be nice to get to know each other better?''

Nice wasn't the word that first came to his mind.

Bad, Cade. You need her.

He didn't want to be reminded of that. But no matter how he might feel, he couldn't forget—without her the foundation would get nothing, nada, zilch. ‘‘What did you have in mind?’’

‘‘We could answer questions or do word associations and see how the other thinks.’’

Shoot me now. It sounded like a wedding shower game or something from one of those torturous speed-dating events. Cade kept working.

‘‘Come on, it’ll be fun.’’

Fun? He was beginning to hate that word.

‘‘Want me to go first?’’ she asked.

He finished tying down the first branch. She handed him another without being asked. At least she didn’t need step-by-step instructions on what to do next. ‘‘Please.’’

‘‘Henry.’’

Cade hoped all the questions would be as easy to answer. ‘‘Eccentric, egomaniac, needs to get a real life.’’

‘‘Your turn,’’ Sterling said.

Cade didn’t want a turn, but he’d agreed to play. At least creativity wasn’t one of the rules. ‘‘Henry.’’

‘‘Happy, fun, rich.’’ She placed a palm on the roof right where it belonged. ‘‘Kids.’’

‘‘Great, incredible, a lot of work.’’ He secured the next branch. ‘‘Kids.’’

‘‘Kisses, hugs, love.’’ She flipped her hair behind her shoulder. Funny, but the motion reminded him of an animal swatting flies with its tail. ‘‘Money.’’

‘‘Evil, corrupt, destroys.’’ He pulled more string from his shorts pocket. At this rate, they might finish before the rain started, but the idea of sharing such a tight space with Sterling made sleeping outside in the rain an appealing option. His muscles tensed. ‘‘Money.’’

She closed her eyes for a moment as if in deep thought then opened them. ‘‘Necessary, important, security.’’

Cade bit back a chuckle. If anything, this little game

proved what he already knew. They were opposites in every sense of the word, but that didn't matter. All they had to do was survive the next fourteen days together and then they would never have to see each other ever again. "We need another row of branches on top of the first one."

Sterling handed him a frond. "Marriage."

The cord he was tying broke. Cade blew out a puff of air. He didn't want to play any longer. "No opinion."

"Everyone has an opinion on marriage."

With a new piece of rope, he tied on the branch. "Not me."

She raised a brow. "Why?"

He took the end of the palm she held, but Sterling wouldn't let go. "Why do you want to get married?" he asked.

A dreamy expression formed on her face. She looked younger, almost innocent. Totally unlike the woman he knew her to be. She released her end of the branch. If his sister ever got her hands on Sterling, Kelsey could make a fortune planning her wedding.

"Marriage makes you a part of something wonderful." Sterling's smile softened even more. "You get security and stability and a family. It doesn't get any better than that."

"Nice fantasy, but don't buy into it." He positioned the palm. "My parents' marriage—make that marriages—have never been like that." His might have been, though. If he hadn't been so stupid.

"My parents' marriage is over-the-top romantic. It's a little…weird how they are so into each other that nothing else matters," she admitted. "There has to exist a happy medium between your parents and mine."

"Maybe."

He thought about Maggie. Maggie Parrish. Once the woman of his dreams. Only she was no longer his. Now she was Maggie Donovan—wife to Jack, mother to Abigail and Benjamin.

"Cade?" Sterling asked.

He secured another branch. "Sorry. What did you say?"

"I said you'll change your mind about marriage once you meet the right person."

"I've already met the perfect woman."

Sterling held a branch as big as she was in mid-air. "Y-you have?"

"Yes, I have."

As he took the branch from her, the edges of her mouth curled. Her grin lit up her flushed, dirty face. She was kind of cute all messed-up with her makeup sweated off.

"And she's the right one?" Sterling asked.

"The only one."

She started to speak, stopped herself and did that fly swatting thing again with her hair. "So what's your next step?"

"There isn't one." He tied the branch to the bamboo frame. That should work. Three layers would be better, but there wasn't time for another complete row.

"Why not?" she asked.

Cade removed a poncho from its package. "Why not what?"

She unfolded her poncho. "Why not take the next step?"

He didn't want to answer and concentrated on covering half the roof with his poncho. He caught her eye. A big mistake. Sterling tapped her toe, waiting for an answer as if she had a right to butt in on his business. She was worse than a rat dog with bows on her ears that wouldn't let go of a bone even though it was too big for her mouth. Might as well answer the question so they could get back to work. ‘‘She’s taken.’’

Sterling dropped her poncho. ‘‘No, she’s not.’’

‘‘Yes, she is.’’ He placed his poncho on the roof and used more branches to hold it down. ‘‘I wanted Maggie to sign a prenuptial agreement before the wedding, but she wouldn’t.’’

‘‘Maggie?’’

‘‘That’s her name.’’

‘‘Oh.’’ Sterling stared at the ground. ‘‘What’s the big deal about signing a pre-nup? You have to protect your assets.’’

Of course, she understood, but Maggie hadn’t. She’d said his wanting her to sign the agreement was a breach of trust and a lack of commitment. That money was more important than their love. She felt signing the pre-nup acknowledged divorce as an option and would set their marriage up for failure. ‘‘It was a big deal to Maggie. We broke up. By the time I realized my mistake, she’d met someone else. She’s married now with kids.’’

Cade remembered the Christmas card he’d received a few months ago. The picture of Maggie’s family had been a left hook to his jaw. Thinking of Maggie as the mother of someone else’s children had been hard. Seeing it in print had been harder. He checked the roof for bare spots. ‘‘I need your poncho.’’

The smile had disappeared from Sterling’s face. She handed him the poncho. ‘‘I’m sorry. I didn’t mean—’’

‘‘It’s okay.’’ He secured the second poncho with more branches. ‘‘You must be tired.’’

‘‘I meant about Maggie.’’

He heard the regret in Sterling’s voice and looked at

her. "You didn't force me to talk about her. I was thinking about Maggie earlier anyway."

"You were?"

He nodded. "She would have loved this island. Her perfect getaway was a two-week backpacking trip in a wilderness area. We'd pack in our supplies and pack out our trash."

"You did this by choice?"

Cade bit back a laugh at the horror in Sterling's voice. "Not at first, but Maggie taught me to love the outdoors."

Sterling paled and concern inched its way down Cade's spine. Exhaustion? It had been a long day.

"You going to be okay?" He hoped she was only tired.

She gave a tight smile. "I'll be fine."

Cade picked up a palm. "We'd better get back to work."

Cynthia stared at the ominous clouds overhead. The scent of rain filled the air, overpowering the smell of the sea. Cade had been right. It was going to rain. Most likely storm. Exactly what she needed to top off this perfectly horrible day.

She picked up the radio and nearly dropped it. Her hands ached, but she couldn't let go. The radio was her only contact to Henry and the outside world.

If the storm turned bad enough, she would demand he come get them. All of this was his fault. Dragging her away from Travis, introducing her to Cade, promising her two weeks of fun in the sun and love on a tropical paradise, setting her up for disappointment. Nothing was working out like she expected.

Not the adventure.

Not the island.

Not even Cade.

She placed the radio in the supply crate. It would stay dry now. Unlike her. She was hurting, dirty, hungry and soon she would be wet. What had Henry been thinking?

He must have lost his mind. Temporary insanity. She couldn't believe he planned all of this on purpose. She understood about Cade, but this island?

Paradise it wasn't. Paradise included waiters to bring you food and drink, air-conditioning and indoor plumbing. With the dark clouds blanketing the sky, there wasn't even a beautiful sunset to admire. Remove the crashing waves, the sea breeze and the salt air and she could easily call it hell.

Her shoulders sagged. She didn't care about the bad posture. That was the least of her problems.

Cade had already found the perfect woman. And not just any perfect woman, either. A wilderness lover who enjoyed camping and backpacking and going to the bathroom outside. Talk about opposites. *Maggie would have loved the island.* Well, Cynthia hated it and couldn't wait to leave. No way would he ever fall in love with her.

That was for sure. She glanced down.

Her hands. Her beautiful hands. Gone. Now they were ugly, covered with cuts and scratches and blisters. Most of her nails were broken. She couldn't look at her hands or she would cry.

"How's it going?" Cade asked.

She took a deep breath and forced a smile. "Fine."

"Almost finished?"

Nodding, Cynthia grabbed the handle of a pan. She struggled not to grimace as a knife-edge pain shot up her arm. She wanted to drop the pan into the crate, but she remembered the radio already in the box and managed to set the pan down gently next to it.

Cade snapped branches in half and carried the pieces

to the woodpile. Her hands still stinging, she took a break and watched him. He was a picture of efficiency. Not a movement or second wasted. A lock of hair fell over his eyes, and he pushed it back. She wanted to be the one to do that. No, she didn't. Well, maybe in her dreams.

Cynthia picked up the first aid kit, but focused her attention on Cade. His torn, stained T-shirt stretched over his muscles. She'd never been attracted to the earthy-sensual-dirty type before. No doubt there had been a good reason for that. She wasn't the outdoor type. Not like Maggie.

Well, Cynthia wouldn't have been stupid enough not to sign the pre-nup. So there.

He tossed branches into the fire pit he'd dug and circled with stones. "We need to go faster."

Not this again. She was working as fast as she could with hands that felt as if they were on fire. Cynthia leaned her head back to stretch her neck. Talk about a taskmaster. He needed to take a break and smell the hibiscus. Of course it didn't help he loved all the outdoor stuff she hated. "It's not raining yet."

"But it will soon."

She felt his gaze on her. He had the most breathtaking eyes. A brilliant blue surrounded by thick, almost luxurious lashes. What she would pay for eyelashes like that. If not for the rugged planes of his face, his eyelashes might make him look feminine. But they didn't. No, they were perfect.

Cynthia wondered why she hadn't noticed them before. And then it hit her. "Where are your glasses?"

Cade lit a match and the fire crackled to life. At least they could warm up a can of beans for dinner. They'd worked through lunch and she was so hungry. Hard to believe canned anything sounded great.

"My what?" he asked.

"Your glasses. You took them off while you were working, but you never put them back on."

"My eyesight's 20/20."

She placed food in the second crate. "Then why do you wear glasses?"

"The coating on the lenses causes glare with flash photography." He picked up their backpacks. "Keeps my picture from being plastered all over."

She laughed. "Good one."

He placed the backpacks inside the shelter. "I'm serious."

His tone wiped the smile from her face. "Really?"

"That's what happens when your middle name makes you tabloid fodder."

"I'm sorry. I didn't—"

"Forget about it," he said. "Are you almost—"

The first drop of rain fell from the sky. And then another. Luckily it was nothing more than a drizzle.

Cade rushed to the crates. "We need to cover them before it gets worse."

The rain actually felt good, but he had a point. Those clouds didn't look like a drizzle was all they had in mind.

Cynthia picked up the crate's cover. The edge scraped her right hand. She doubled over, but held on to the lid.

Cade fastened the top on the other supply crate. "What's wrong?"

"Nothing." Somehow she got the lid on. Blood dripped from her hand, leaving a palm print on the crate. Maybe Cade wouldn't notice…

He draped the plastic tarp over the top of the two crates. "Lift the corner of the crate so we can secure it."

She struggled, but managed to do it.

"What the hell—heck is wrong with your hands?"

He'd noticed. She hid her hands behind her back. "A cut."

Water clung to his hair. "Show me."

Maybe if she pretended she didn't hear him…

"Sterling."

Before she could do anything, the floodgates of heaven opened. Rain fell hard and fast.

"Damn," Cade said. "Go inside."

The three unsecured tarp edges flapped around. "The tarp."

"I'll take care of it," Cade said.

She hesitated. The rain pelted her. The drops got bigger with each passing second.

"Get under cover."

Her hands hurt so much she knew she wasn't much help anyway. She ran to the lean-to and crawled in.

The tight, dark quarters reminded her of when she and her parents had to live out of their car, and Cynthia wished she could be outside even if it meant getting drenched in the rain.

A flashlight lay near the entrance and she turned it on. As she scooted farther in, a palm poked her shoulder. She aimed the flashlight around. Palm branches covered three sides and the roof. Not much head room. Leg or elbow room, either. The bamboo floor was hard and uncomfortable even with the canvas cloth covering it.

Water dripped from her. Blood, too. She didn't think there could be a place worse than the island torture she'd experienced all day, but she'd found it.

Cade made his way into the shelter, making the space more crowded and claustrophobic. Come tomorrow they needed to remodel. Who was she kidding? Come tomorrow, she was gone.

Cade held the first aid kit and the bottle of gin.

A drink. She needed one. ‘‘You forgot the olives.’’

He frowned. ‘‘We’re not having martinis. The gin is to sterilize the cut. There’s no alcohol in the first aid kit, but we can use the gauze to wrap your hand.’’

Hand. He didn’t realize both of her hands were hurt. She placed them on her lap. ‘‘I can do it myself.’’

‘‘I’ll do it.’’ He rolled up one edge of the canvas floor covering. Not that it mattered since everything was getting wet. Maybe he didn’t want the place to smell like gin. ‘‘Let me see your hands.’’

She placed her hands palm down over the uncovered portion of the flooring.

‘‘Turn them over.’’

Cade’s tone told her he wasn’t kidding around. Slowly she did. Red and peeling blisters dotted her fingers and palms. Scratches marred her once smooth skin. And blood. Dripping on the floor, down her hand, everywhere.

Cade took one look and closed his eyes.

She turned off the flashlight. ‘‘My hands are so gross they’re making you sick.’’

He didn’t answer. That made it worse. Sitting in the darkness with the rain pounding the roof and sides of the shelter, Cynthia felt her dreams disappear, washed away like a message in a bottle by the ebbing tide. She was destined to be an old maid and spend the rest of her life alone with no one to love her except her parents’ cats. And once they died…

‘‘It’s not you.’’

She looked at him, but it was too dark to see his face. ‘‘What do you mean?’’

‘‘I have a slight issue with…blood.’’

She turned on the flashlight and directed the beam at him. His eyes were still closed. He looked a little pale. ‘‘What kind of issue?’’

''It's nothing.''

''No, it's something.'' She wasn't the only one with a weakness. They had something in common. She clung to this glimmer of hope like a baby to her mother. It was all she had left except a future of loneliness and cat food. ''I've heard about interns who faint at the sight of blood—''

''I don't faint.'' He opened his eyes and his pupils dilated. ''I can handle a little blood. But when my sister, Kelsey, was six, she cut her chin on the diving board. There was so much blood. In the water. On her.''

''So it's just a lot of blood you can't handle?''

''I hate needles, too. But it's not a problem.'' He looked at her hands. ''See? Not a big deal. Ready?''

She nodded and he dribbled the gin on her hands. It stung. Cynthia gasped, but she didn't cry. If Cade could handle seeing blood, she could handle the pain and smelling like a seedy bar.

''Let them air dry,'' he said. ''How do they feel?''

''Fine.''

He raised a brow.

''They sting a little,'' she admitted. ''But no big deal.''

''You should have stopped working once you got a blister.''

''I wanted to do my share of the work.''

As he studied her, her heart sunk to her feet. Of course he was disappointed with her. She wasn't like Maggie, who probably would have built the shelter all by herself using dental floss without breaking either a sweat or a fingernail. Cynthia was a total failure at this outdoor adventure stuff, at being an attractive woman. She imagined what Cade saw when he looked at her. Bad hair, no makeup, dirt, scratches, bloody hands.

She might as well face the truth. Cade saw it.

"I'm ugly. I know." A weight lifted as she spoke the words she'd been feeling all afternoon, almost all her life. "My hands, my hair, everything."

"Give me a break, Sterling, you couldn't be ugly if you tried."

He only wanted to make her feel better. People, especially men, would say anything to get what they wanted. And Cade seemed to love everything about this damned island. Well, naive she wasn't. "You're just saying that," she said. "Look at me."

Cade did. He took a long, hard look.

Sterling sat cross-legged and rested her hands on her lap. She was more drowned rat than beauty queen with wet hair plastered to her head, but some strands were also tousled like she'd just stepped from the shower. He liked it much better this way than how it looked combed and brushed with sprays and gels to keep it under control and in place.

Sterling's face looked better, too. No layers of makeup to hide beneath. Dirty and rain-streaked with scratches, she looked natural, more like the girl-next-door with freckles on her cheeks and nose than a pristine society miss with blemish-free skin.

Her body was that of a centerfold model. Wet clothes clung to her like a second skin, leaving nothing about her body to his imagination. Her Capri pants melded to her hips and thighs, accentuating each curve and inch of toned muscle. Her white top was so transparent he saw the intricate lace pattern on her bra. And her breasts… If he kept looking he would need to be doused by rain again to cool off.

Cade forced his attention to her hands. Her once clean, soft, fragile hands and manicured, polished nails had been replaced with scratched and blistered skin and broken, dirt-encrusted fingernails. Okay, her hands were pretty gross, but they'd gotten that way because of her determination to help out. He doubted if she'd ever done a hard day's labor before, yet she'd continued working though the pain of her hands. That in itself was something beautiful.

"So?" she asked.

"You're not ugly," he answered.

"How can you say that?"

"It's the truth."

"But I'm a mess."

She reminded him of his sister Kelsey after her confidence had taken one too many dings. Good thing he had lots of big brother training. "Only because you worked hard today. Not many people could have done what you did. You didn't quit and that's more attractive than a made-up face or styled hair."

Sterling stared at him as if she wanted to contradict him, but slowly the edges of her mouth curled. "Thanks."

That was almost too easy. "You're welcome."

A gust of wind rattled the lean-to. The rain intensified, falling faster and harder. The drops sounded like taps on a snare drum. She shivered.

"Cold?" he asked.

She nodded. "I keep trying to picture myself on some tropical island where it's warm and sunny, but then I realize I'm already here."

Cade smiled. She wasn't so bad. "You'll feel better if you change into dry clothes."

"I..."

"What's wrong?"

She looked down at her hands. "I don't think I can

undress myself. They still hurt. But it's okay. I'm not that cold."

Goose bumps covered her arms. She continued shivering. The sooner she was out of her clothes, the better. "I'll help you."

She smiled, almost shyly. "Thanks."

Don't thank me yet.

Cade stared at her full breasts. He had doubts he could do this. *You have to.* And he would. He couldn't forget this was Sterling. He didn't like her. He wasn't attracted to her. Okay, maybe a little, but she was soaking wet. It was only natural. Whatever he felt was strictly physical. Too bad undressing her was a strictly physical act.

Not that anything physical would happen between them. It wouldn't. It couldn't. This was only about making sure Sterling didn't get sick. He needed her to stay healthy so she could make it to the end. Nothing else mattered. Not her incredible body. Not the gleam of anticipation in her eyes.

And if he believed that, he'd better reply to the e-mail offering to sell him a map to locate the fountain of youth in Florida.

"There's a long-sleeved T-shirt and black leggings in my backpack. I don't have anything warmer."

"You can wear my sweatshirt." The more clothes she had on, the better. He reached into her pack and pulled out a thong, nothing more than a wisp of pink fabric. Blood drained from his head. What had he expected her to wear? Full-coverage generic white panties?

"Don't worry." Amusement twinkled in her eyes. "I won't make you put those on me."

"Thanks," Cade said, but he wasn't so sure. If she didn't need new panties was she going to wear the ones she had on or go without? His groin tightened.

"I don't need a bra, either."

She was killing him, a slow, tortuous death. He should be complaining more, but he knew she wasn't doing this on purpose. Still knowing that didn't make his task less difficult. He found the clothes she wanted.

Sterling turned so her back faced him. "Will this work?"

She wasn't stupid. Neither was he. "This works much better." Especially for him. Maybe he'd better start dating more if a woman like Sterling could have this reaction on him. "I'll point the flashlight away."

"Thank you."

"I can close my eyes."

She laughed, the warm sound added a couple of degrees to his already increasing temperature. "That's a sweet thought, but unnecessary. We're both adults."

That's what he was afraid of. Yes, he'd been spending too much time at the office and not socializing enough.

As he reached around her to undo her shirt buttons, his palm brushed the side of her breast. She drew in a quick breath.

Aw, hell. Heck. "I didn't mean—"

"It's okay."

It was far from okay. Okay didn't begin to describe how stimulating that nanosecond of a touch had been. What was he thinking? This wasn't foreplay. This was Sterling. Pampered, spoiled Sterling. But she wasn't, not really. He was starting to see another side to her. And liking it. Liking her.

But he couldn't forget one crucial point.

This was all about survival. His, hers, Smiling Moon's.

Time to get down to business. As Cade mentally recited the Greek and Latin alphabets, he unbuttoned her blouse, peeled the fabric off her shoulders and arms and laid the shirt out to dry. There, that wasn't so bad. He reached for her T-shirt.

"My bra is wet."

No kidding. And much better wet than dry.

She glanced back, her face half-hidden by her bare shoulder. "It, uh, fastens in the front. I—I can try—"

"I'll do it."

Cade finished what he started. It wasn't as if he hadn't done this before. Under other circumstances…

His fingertips brushed her breast. Soft, warm, feminine. Blood rushed where he didn't want it to go, but he found the clasp. His hand lingered. Temptation was calling. Dare he answer?

The rapid pounding of her heart matched his. His fingers froze. He was straddling Heaven and Hell. It could go either way. If he moved his hand over to the right or to the left—

"Do you need help?" she asked.

He unclasped her bra and it sprung open. "I got it."

And boy, did he want it.

He eased the straps over her shoulders and down her arms. The gesture seemed so familiar, so natural, but the action was the most unnatural thing he'd ever done.

There was *something* between them. Physical chemistry. That's all it could be.

He almost tossed her shirt to her until he realized she wouldn't be able to catch it or put it on herself. He grabbed the shirt and glanced her way.

Smooth, soft, pale skin.

Close your eyes now.

But he couldn't. He was only staring at her back, but he didn't want to look away. Her skin glowed in the subtle light. She'd pushed her hair over to one side and in front of her shoulder giving him a great view of the curve of her neck, the line of her shoulders and her back tapering to her waist. As beautiful as Venus de Milo with its pearly white luminescence, Sterling was a work of art herself. He could have stared at her all night.

She shivered. "Cade? Did you get lost?"

"The shirt," he said finally and put it on her. He helped her into his sweatshirt. Cade felt off-centered, but he managed to get her out of her pants and into her leggings without making a total fool of himself. Closing his eyes had helped. So did reciting sexual harassment legal statutes.

"Aren't you going to change?" she asked.

He needed to cool off. "I'll grab us something to eat."

She grinned. A good sign. "Don't forget the coffee. That'll warm us right up."

He glanced outside at the pouring rain. "The fire's out."

Her smile disappeared. "But…"

Wind ripped through the camp making a sound that would scare goblins on Halloween. The entire structure shook, but none of the branches blew off.

With her pale skin and wide eyes, Sterling looked lost and afraid. He wanted to pull her onto his lap and make her feel better, but that wasn't an option. Not now, not ever. Cade tapped one side of the lean-to. "The shelter might not look like much, but it'll make it through the night."

She drew her knees to her chest. "What about us?"

"We'll be fine." He covered her with the almost dry blanket. "Once you eat—"

Drops of water hit his forehead. "Dam—darn, the roof's leaking."

He grabbed a sock out of his backpack and shoved it into the branches to stop the water from dripping inside.

More leaks appeared. Cade stuffed clothing into the branches to stop the water flow, but couldn't keep up.

Another gust hit the shelter. More water seeped inside landing right on top of Sterling.

"That's it," she announced. "It's useless."

He stuck a pair of his underwear in between the branches. "It'll be okay."

"No, it won't." Her bottom lip quivered. "I'm wet. I'm cold. I'm hungry and my hands hurt. I've tried to do this. I really have, but I've never been so miserable in all my life."

He understood her frustration. He felt that way, too.

"It's going to get better. In the morning—"

"Forget about morning, I want Henry to come get me *now.*"

Chapter Five

The look in Cade's eyes made Cynthia feel an eighth of an inch tall. "If it's too dangerous for Henry to come get me tonight, I'll leave in the morning."

"It's too dangerous."

With the downpour assaulting the lean-to like miniature cannonballs, she knew Cade would say that. She hugged her knees, careful of her hands.

"It's not so bad," Cade said.

She glanced up at the ceiling. Water dribbled through the palms and clothing. "Any minute the shelter is going to blow away. It'll be a miracle if I survive tonight."

"Where's your sense of adventure?"

He sounded disappointed. She pretended not to care and held on to her resolve to leave. "Trying a new restaurant that hasn't been reviewed or flying coach. Those are my kind of adventures."

"If that's true, you haven't lived."

"I've lived plenty." She was not going to be swayed by a pretty face or a killer smile or beautiful blue eyes or any kind of rationale he might come up with. In fact, it bothered her he just sat here. She'd told him she was hungry. He should be getting food. And what about the radio? They needed to check in with Henry. She was being unreasonable, but everything about this adventure was unreasonable.

"So what do you say, Sterling?" Cade asked.

"Why do you call me Sterling? Did you forget my name?"

Her questions seemed to surprise him. "Your name is Cynthia, but Sterling fits you better. You're like a piece of silver. Elegant, polished."

Another time, another place she would have loved to hear those words. But not now. Not here. Not from him.

"You don't like me very much, do you?"

He furrowed his brow. "I don't know you well enough not to like you. Would you rather I call you Cynthia?"

She shrugged. "You can call me whatever you want."

"Then I'll call you Sterling."

She didn't care. By this time tomorrow she would be asleep in her cabin on Henry's yacht sailing back to civilization. And her stomach wouldn't be growling and threatening to mutiny in order to get food. She couldn't wait to be clean, dry and warm.

"Tell me you'll stay." He spoke softly, his words a gentle caress, as his hands had been when he undressed her. "We have a great opportunity to spend the next fourteen days here. Alone." Cade emphasized the last word and her heart beat triple time.

Yes, he was gorgeous, intelligent and rich. He didn't seem to mind that she looked like something out of a horror movie, either, which totally boggled her mind. But they weren't for each other. Not when he could send her pulse quickening or her heart pounding or her nerve endings dancing with an innocent touch. He was right. They hardly knew each other. She shouldn't be feeling this way with him. "I can't stay."

"Think about all you would give up if you quit."

She wasn't giving up anything except a living nightmare. "I want to go home."

"You won't win your reward."

"It's probably an expensive bauble. I have enough of those."

"You'll never be invited to Henry's birthday parties."

She'd thought about that. "Henry and I are too close. He would invite me no matter what."

"His rules were quite clear."

Cade sounded like such an attorney. He would be a good politician. Too bad she wouldn't be the one standing at his side. "Rules are meant to be broken. Especially Henry's rules."

"If he doesn't enforce the rules, his adventures become meaningless."

Cynthia knew how important the adventures were to Henry. That made them important to her. She bit her lip. The idea of never attending one of his parties—or worse, hurting his feelings and losing his friendship—left a void within her. One she didn't know how she would fill.

Cade opened his backpack and pulled out a bottle of pills. "Would you like any for your hands?"

"No, thanks."

"Suit yourself." He downed two without any water.

"What's wrong?" she asked.

He rubbed his temples. "A headache."

"What can I do to help?"

"Stay."

No way was *she* his best medicine. Something else was going on. "Why is my staying so important to you?"

His gaze locked with hers and her breath caught in her throat. ''If you leave, I don't get my reward.''

She almost laughed. It was funny and sad at the same time. He wasn't interested in her. Only what he could get from her. He was no different than a million other guys. She should have known. ''What's so special about your reward?''

''You wouldn't understand.''

He'd slammed the door without giving her a chance and it hurt. ''How can you say that? You admitted you didn't know me.''

''I know women like you.''

''Maggie?''

He laughed. ''No.''

Cynthia had asked for that one. ''You shouldn't be so quick to judge.''

''Perhaps,'' he said. ''You have lasted longer than I thought you would.''

A backhanded compliment, but she *was* still here. That was an accomplishment no matter how miserable she felt. ''So tell me about your reward.''

''Henry will make a donation to the foundation I run.''

Cade ran a foundation and was a lawyer, too. Impressive. The strains of ''Hail to the Chief'' played in her head. But she didn't understand why he couldn't see the obvious. ''If you only need donations, why don't we both write checks to the foundation? It gets the money and we can leave the island.''

''Henry pledged five million dollars annually if we stay on the island for two weeks.''

''Oh.'' She didn't have that kind of money. Not many people did. Leave it to Henry. ''So what does your foundation do?''

''Smiling Moon helps kids—all sorts of children, but

the at-risk kids are the ones who need us the most. It's important I get Henry's donation.''

''Where did the name Smiling Moon come from?''

''I worked as a guardian ad litem, a children's advocate. There was a little girl named Bethany who kept staring out the window one night. I asked what she was looking at and she answered the man in the moon. Bethany said she'd heard he smiled, but she had only seen him frown. It stuck with me.''

And Cynthia wanted to stick with him. A warm glow settled in the center of her chest at the thought of Cade and Bethany. He had such a caring, good heart. ''I'm sure it did.''

''You can't imagine what these kids have gone through.''

As Cynthia listened to his heart-wrenching stories, she saw another side to Cade. She knew lots of philanthropists, but for him it was a calling. She heard it in his voice; she saw it in his eyes. He wasn't interested in only making money; he wanted to make the world a better place for kids. His foundation was a way to make that happen, and his dedication shed a new light on him. Cade had a purpose in life. She respected that. Envied it, too.

He continued. ''A lot of these kids have no one to look out for them. They're starved for love, for attention. Good or bad. It's impossible for you to understand how these kids feel—''

''I understand more than you think,'' she admitted. His words touched a chord deep within her. Even as an adult, she felt a little like those kids he'd described.

''How?'' Disbelief sounded in his voice. ''You've never wanted for anything in your entire life.''

Oh, yes, she had. Just thinking about it made her stomach knot. She felt clammy. ''Those kids might want the latest athletic shoes or hottest CD, but it's not about getting material things. It's about feeling safe, having a sense of belonging and being loved."

Three things she'd wanted to feel all her life. Three things she was still searching for today. Someday she would find them. Maybe she already had. She stared at Cade.

"No one else..." He studied her with a disconcerting look in his eyes. "I never thought someone like you would understand."

"Someone like me..." She looked away.

"I judged you too quickly."

But he had been partially correct about her. She was concerned about things others would call frivolous—clothes, hair, makeup. Things that didn't matter to the kids needing Smiling Moon's help. Things that didn't seem to matter to Cade.

He was...different. Cynthia could see that now. He cared so much about a bunch of kids, strangers. His compassion, devotion, generosity would carry over to his own family—to his wife and children. A lump the size of a wedding cake formed in her throat.

"I'm sorry," he said. "I was wrong."

And so was she. She'd been wrong about so many things.

But the first was Cade Armstrong Waters. For so long she'd been searching and she'd finally found him. He was the one.

Her one.

And perfect or not, she knew what she had to do. She had to help him realize his dream and get the reward for Smiling Moon. It was too important to him for her to say no. "I'll stay."

* * *

Morning brought a cloudless blue sky and sunshine, but the storm had wreaked havoc on the island. Cade didn't care. Nor did he care that he hadn't slept at all last night. As he gathered the mangos and grapefruit littering the camp with branches and leaves, he fought the urge to whistle.

Sterling was staying.

All his hopes and dreams for making Smiling Moon a success had rested on her. She hadn't disappointed him. Instead she'd surprised him by her willingness to remain on the island and her understanding of the kids he wanted to help. For so many years, he tried to explain it to his parents and sister. They understood to a point, but in just a few minutes, Sterling had gotten it. She wasn't the kind of woman who should care let alone understand. That both confused and intrigued him. These next two weeks could be more interesting than he originally thought.

"Good morning." Sterling, wearing a pair of shorts and a tank top, crawled out of the lean-to. He caught a glimpse of a white strap. She'd managed to put on a bra.

Cade picked up a coconut. "How are your hands?"

"Better." She motioned to her clothing. "I dressed myself."

It bothered him that he wanted to be the one dressing her. "Want me to change the bandages?"

"No, thanks, but do you know how to braid hair?"

He'd tried braiding his sister's hair once. Just thinking about trying to do that with Sterling made his stomach clench. The last thing he need to do was run his fingers through her hair. Though he imagined it would be more tangles than silky strands after getting caught in the rainstorm. Still… He was putting way too much thought into this. "I'm not a hair braider, but I make a mean breakfast."

"Good thing, because I'm starving." She wet her lips. "What's on the menu this morning?"

He raised a mango in one hand and a grapefruit in the other. "Fresh fruit plate."

Her eyes widened. "Where did those come from?"

"Compliments of the storm." He motioned to the trees. "We're surrounded by fruit trees so we won't starve."

"And we won't have to worry about scurvy either."

He smiled, rinsed off a mango and tossed it to her. "There's coffee, too."

She poured herself a cup and took a sip. "It isn't Jamaican Blue Mountain, but it will do."

He dropped a clean mango in the sand. "Damn. Er, darn."

"Why do you keep stopping yourself from swearing? Hell or damn aren't that bad of words."

"I made a promise to the kids at Smiling Moon."

"You're devoted to them, aren't you?"

"Someone has to be."

A horn blasted.

"Henry." She set her mug on a log and ran toward the beach.

Cade followed, wondering why he hadn't received such an enthusiastic good morning.

Henry waded to shore. In his pressed khaki shorts and whiter than white camp shirt, he looked as if he'd walked off the pages of a travel brochure. As soon as he hit the beach, Sterling hugged him. "Thank goodness you're here."

Henry Davenport's roguish smile had made him infamous with the ladies. Right now, he might as well be the devil since Cade would sell his soul for the donation. "Rough night, darling?"

"You have no idea," she said. "Look at my hands."

Henry frowned. ''Are you okay?''

She nodded. ''But my hair…''

''You look beautiful, natural.'' He combed a strand away from her face. ''Good morning, Cade.''

There was nothing good about it. He didn't like how chummy Henry acted with Sterling. Friends were one thing, but the way he touched her hair… Cade picked up a seashell and tossed it into the water. ''It's better than last night.''

''Quite a storm.'' Henry whistled. ''Not a fun night.''

''We survived,'' Cade said. ''Didn't we, Sterling?''

''Yes, we did.'' She straightened her shoulders. ''So now that you're here, Henry, are we going to play some games?''

Henry grinned and assumed his pretty boy reality TV game show host persona. ''I'm happy you're so excited to play.''

''You know me,'' Sterling said. ''Always up for an adventure.''

She winked at Cade. He had to give her credit for trying.

''Follow me and I'll explain the rules.'' Henry led them along a narrow path through the palm trees and verdant green bushes. ''It's quite simple. There are five bowls. If you eat a bite from each bowl, you win.''

''What do we win?'' she asked.

''The winners pick a prize from the luxury chest I brought with me. The chest is filled with all sorts of goodies picked out by *moi.* Practical items like cooking utensils and supplies, various sundry items and some not-so-practical items like pillows and clothing.'' Henry rubbed his chin. ''I'll toss in a bonus prize and allow the winners to join me for lunch. But the losers get what they deserve—nothing.''

Cade worried about Sterling. If she lost, her feelings would be hurt. She'd agreed to stay, but he wondered for how long. He had to make sure she was happy and comfortable so she would last until the end. "Isn't that a little harsh?"

Henry shrugged. "Life is harsh."

Not Henry's life. Harsh meant no one picking up his dry cleaning or turning down his sheets at night. Henry Davenport was too spoiled by the good life. He would never survive one night, let alone fourteen, on this island.

"Oh, I forgot one thing." Henry smiled. "The person eating will be blindfolded so the other must feed them."

"That could be—" she raised a brow "—fun."

Sounded more like trouble with a capital *T*. Especially since Cade was warming up to her. Hel—heck, he was starting to like her though he chalked that up to her agreeing to stay on the island. But his attraction to her last night confused him. It must have been an anomaly due to the storm, the crowded confines, her amazing body. No other explanation made sense. He was here for the donation only. Anything else was out of the question and a complication he didn't want or need.

Henry led them to a clearing surrounded by bushes and towering trees. Cade heard the sound of waves crashing on the beach, but he couldn't see the water and he wondered how Henry had managed to set this up. Had the crew come with him? He couldn't have done this alone.

A table was set with two place settings of fine china and flatware. In the center were five bowls. Bugs flew around and landed on the food. Inside the bowls, squishy, squirmy things tried to slime their way out.

"Snack time," Henry said.

Sterling leaned against Cade. "I'm going to be sick."

Cade put his arm around her. "Look away."

''You can forfeit your right to play if you choose,'' Henry announced. ''But if you do, no prize or lunch.''

''I forfeit,'' she said without a moment's hesitation. ''I'll never be that hungry.''

Cade didn't want to do this either. Henry had gone too far this time. ''I forfeit, too.''

Henry frowned. ''But—''

''No buts allowed.'' Sterling placed her hands on her hips, and Cade was so proud of her. ''I can't believe you're doing this to us. To me. The island is bad enough, but this silly little game of yours…'' She sighed. ''I thought you cared about me.''

''I do care,'' Henry explained. ''I only want to make you happy.''

''You have a strange way of showing it.''

Henry's eyes narrowed. ''What will make you happy?''

Cade's stomach knotted. She was going to ask to leave.

Instead she tilted her chin. ''If one of us eats from the five bowls, we not only get a luxury item, the Smiling Moon Foundation gets this island and your yacht so they can bring the kids here for summer camp.''

Sterling's spunk blew Cade away. He hadn't expected this. She wanted to help the kids—his kids—by giving them this island. True, it was a pie-in-the-sky request, but the motivation behind her asking… Could he have been so wrong about her?

Henry looked at her, then at Cade. ''Okay.''

Cade's heart skipped a beat. ''You agree? To everything?''

Henry nodded. ''As long as one of you completes the game.''

''I'll eat,'' Cade said without an ounce of hesitation. ''Once you put the island and yacht donation in writing.''

''Cynthia must feed you,'' Henry said.

She took a step back, but Cade wouldn't let her move any farther away. "I can't do it."

"Yes, you can, Sterling." Cade gave her a reassuring squeeze and pretended not to notice how nice it felt to have his arm around her. "Think about the kids spending the summer on the island. And it will all be because of you."

"But I don't want to touch…" She grimaced. "Just the thought makes my stomach turn."

"Can she use a fork to feed me?" he asked.

Henry studied the two of them. "Yes, I've modified the prize so I can modify the rules to allow that."

"You're so generous." And eccentric and too rich for his own good. But if Cade got hold of this island… He grinned. "You don't have to touch anything except the fork. Okay?"

She nodded, but looked more green than confident. "Are you sure about this?"

Cade had never been more sure of anything. "Yes, but it's going to take a team effort to get it done."

"Keep going. You're doing great."

Cade's encouragement kept Cynthia going. That and an empty stomach. The centipede or banana slug or whatever it was squirmed at the end of her fork. It would have been better for Cade if she stabbed the worm with the tines, but she couldn't. She'd agreed to stay on the island. She'd agreed to play this game without the chance to win a luxury item or lunch. The kids were worth it. Cade was worth it. But she drew the line at killing anything, even an icky, squishy worm, for him.

She'd come a long way in only twenty-four hours, but not that far. Still, she was here. An amazing feat in itself. She'd taken one look at herself in the mirror this morning and made a decision—no mirrors for the next two weeks. Already her hair was greasy and tangled. Disgusting actually. Her face needed an oatmeal and goat milk scrub, only that container had been left on the ship to make room for the food she took from the galley. Too bad a mirror wasn't necessary to see her hands. But she didn't have it as bad as the worm on the end of her fork or Cade.

She stared at Cade. A blindfold hid his eyes. Stubble covered the lower portion of his face and made him look more rugged.

"You're doing awesome," he said.

Her? Awesome? Her cheeks warmed.

"Last one—" One more gulp and the game would be over. Thank goodness. She couldn't believe he'd eaten from the other four bowls. She assumed he was swallowing the things whole, just like he'd done with the pills last night. She still shuddered at the thought. "Open wide and swallow."

"You sound like you enjoy saying that," Cade said.

"Yes, it's a real turn-on to feed gross things to a man."

Cade's smile took her by surprise. A lot of what he did surprised her and she liked that about him. She liked a lot of things about him. He opened his mouth.

This was it. Her hand trembled as she brought the fork to his lips. He only grimaced slightly as the worm went down, whipped his blindfold off and guzzled a tall glass of water.

"You win," Henry announced.

Cade pumped his fist. He jumped off his stool and hugged her. "We did it, Sterling. We did it."

We, not *I.*

She could get used to hearing that. She leaned into the

hug, into him. His chest was solid, his arms strong. He held her. This was where she belonged. The kids just got the island.

And she would get Cade.

Chapter Six

That afternoon, Cade sat on the beach with Sterling. Things were looking up. She had come through when it counted. Smiling Moon had an island and yacht. Cade had a fishing pole and hooks. A little caviar for bait, and he would be catching fish like crazy.

Maybe a fish fry would make Sterling smile. As she watched Henry and his crew prepare for the next game, she drew her lips into a thin line. She raised her sunglasses. "Are those rafts?"

"And oars. Looks like a raft race."

"In the water?"

Cade laughed. "We wouldn't get far rowing on the sand."

"How was your lunch?"

He didn't hear any envy or anger in Sterling's voice, but she seemed anxious. No sense telling her about the delicious French Dip sandwich, chef salad, fruit kabobs and brownie. "It was okay. Did you eat?"

"Yes."

Before he could ask what, Henry announced it was game time. Cade followed Sterling to a line running parallel to the shoreline. Henry stood beside one-person inflatable rafts, life jackets and oars.

"Man vs. nature," Henry said. "We've read the classic tales about man's struggle against nature. Out here, you live it. Last night's storm showed us how powerful an opponent weather can be. It strikes without warning. This afternoon you will battle another force of nature—the sea." Henry handed each a life jacket. "Buoys have been set up for each of you. Blue for Cade. Red for Cynthia. You must row to the buoy, pick up your flag, return to the beach and drag your raft across the finish line."

Cade shielded his eyes from the sun and located his buoy with the blue flag about one hundred yards out.

"If you both complete the race, you may select three items from the luxury chest." Henry narrowed his eyes. "If only one of you finishes the race, you only get one item. Any questions?"

Cade buckled his lifejacket. "I'm ready."

"What about you, Cynthia?" Henry asked.

Sterling tightened a strap on her life vest, but she looked pale. Cade remembered her not wanting to get wet when they arrived on the island and her questions about the raft. He couldn't believe she had a problem getting wet after last night, but she looked tense. He didn't like it. "It'll be fun."

Nodding, she blew out a puff of air.

Henry held a green flag. "On your mark, get set, go."

Cade grabbed his raft, ran with it into the water and hopped in. He glanced back. Sterling stood at the edge of the water with her raft. "Come on," he yelled.

"My hands." She dropped the raft. "It's up to you."

Cade focused on his goal—the buoy with the blue flag.

He struggled to find a rhythm with the oars. Rowing against the waves was hard. He reached the buoy, grabbed his flag and circled back. When he neared the shore, he jumped out and dragged the raft across the finish line.

Water dripped into his eyes. He pushed the wet hair back and looked around. Henry kneeled next to Sterling. "You win one item from the luxury chest, Cade," he said.

"What happened?" Cade asked.

"It hurt too much to carry the raft. No way could I row."

Tears glimmered in Sterling's eyes, but not one fell. She must be in pain. Her bottom lip trembled. Da—darn Henry. Cade shouldn't care as much as he did. He barely knew her.

"Congrats," she said. "I'm sorry I couldn't do the race. Three luxury items would have been nice."

"We can win them tomorrow."

"I need to get back to the ship," Henry said. "Come with me to the boat and pick a prize. Then I'll see the two of you bright and early in the morning."

Cade wanted the snorkel and fins he'd seen earlier. They would help him if he couldn't catch fish with his pole and there were also shellfish to be trapped. Digging through the box, he thought about Sterling. She'd had zero chance of competing with her injured hands. He glimpsed a flash of pink plastic and remembered something else he'd seen this morning in the chest.

As Henry's boat motored away, Cade walked back to Sterling, who sat on the beach and stared at the water. "What did you select?"

"These." He dropped a pair of pink flip-flops in front of her. "I hope they're your size."

Her mouth formed a perfect *O.* "For me?"

He nodded. "Pink isn't my color."

"You could have chosen anything in the chest yet you picked these for me?" She made it sound like a bigger deal than it was.

"We're teammates," he said. "You can't run around in bare feet for the next two weeks."

"Thank you." Her grin lit up her face, and he felt a little tug on his heart. "This is the nicest thing anyone has ever done for me."

Cade doubted that. "You staying on the island is the nicest thing anyone's done for me, not to mention getting the island and yacht for the kids. So we're even, okay?"

Everything was better than okay. While Cade prepared dinner, Cynthia sat on a log watching the sunset. The setting sun cast a surreal glow on the water. Pinks and oranges bled into the deepening blue sky as if blended with the skillful paintbrush of one of the master painters.

Yes, everything was wonderful. She was still dirty and needed to wash her hair, but her hands didn't hurt as much and she wasn't cold and wet. Definite improvements over the hardships she'd endured yesterday.

Even Cade had improved.

Teammate, partner, spouse—a three-step progression of her intended relationship with him. Too bad they couldn't skip the first two steps, but he seemed to do things by the book and play by the rules. Must be the lawyer in him.

As she stared at her new flip-flops, joy filled her heart. She had a closetful of designer shoes, but without a doubt these pink rubber flip-flops would always be her favorite pair. Someday she would tell their children and grandchildren about her first gift from Cade.

He placed a plate of beans, rice and fish on her lap. "Dinner is served."

"Thanks." She couldn't believe Cade had caught a fish for dinner and knew how to clean and prepare it, too. Besides squeezing a filet with lemon and adding a butter sauce and capers, she was clueless about fish. He was going to be the best husband. "It looks great."

"There's more if you're hungry."

He took such good care of her. His caring would soon turn into loving. Maggie would be a distant memory. Just a pothole on the road to everlasting love and a happy ending.

Cynthia took a bite. "It's delicious, but I'm sorry you had to do all the work tonight."

"Your hands will heal soon."

Guilt lodged in her throat. She'd been too frightened to go into the water on the raft and her hands gave her an easy out. "I'm sure they'll be fine tomorrow."

"Don't worry if they aren't." His mouth curved with tenderness. "You're doing your share."

But she wasn't. She hadn't eaten the worms. She hadn't rowed in the raft race. She hadn't cooked dinner.

Some teammate she was turning out to be. It wasn't right, especially if they were to have a future together. She took a deep breath and exhaled slowly. "There's something I need to say."

His fork clattered against his metal plate. "You aren't leaving, are you?"

"Of course, I'm not leaving." She wanted to tell him the truth about the raft race, but all she could think about was Maggie, the wonder outdoorswoman. Cynthia bet Maggie wasn't afraid of the water. She probably wrestled great whites for fun. "It's just…"

Cade leaned toward Cynthia. "What?"

"I, um, I love my new shoes." She'd wanted to be honest with him, but the words wouldn't come. A sense of inadequacy had swept over her. She didn't want Cade to think less of her. "Thank you."

"You already thanked me."

She was such a chicken, the latest and greatest version of the cowardly lion. "I wanted to do it again."

"I'm happy you like them."

"I do. Like them, that is." She was so pathetic. She swallowed a spoonful of rice. "So good."

He raised a brow. "Bet you say that to all of the guys."

"No," she admitted. "Only the ones who let me feed them icky, squishy things."

The next morning, Cade didn't know which was funnier—Henry's pith helmet or his safari outfit. At least he was having fun and getting into the spirit of his adventure.

Henry stood next to a basket containing spears and arrows. Thirty feet down the beach were two targets with multicolored rings surrounding a red bull's-eye.

"Water is the key to survival on the island, but food is also necessary." Henry adjusted his helmet. "During yesterday's game, we saw how the island can provide basic nourishment with unconventional food sources. But there's more than one way to get food from the island."

"Let's hope so." Cade wasn't about to eat another worm.

"I'm counting on it," Sterling said.

"Today's game will test your hunting abilities," Henry explained.

She placed her hands on her hips. "I'm a vegetarian."

"I know that's not true, darling. Beef Wellington is one of your favorites," Henry said. "Don't worry, I won't make you kill anything."

"Thank goodness," she murmured.

Cade laughed. Sterling had a good heart. A good sense

of humor, too. Last night had been fun. She wasn't the most eloquent of speakers, but the way she stumbled over words and made such a big deal of thanking him for her new shoes was sweet.

Still, she wasn't that sweet. He'd had to make sure he didn't touch her when they crawled into the shelter to sleep. Being so close to her was too tempting when he knew how soft and warm she was.

"Today's competition has two parts." Henry picked up a spear. "First, we're going to test your accuracy with a spear. The rules are simple. If you hit the target, you get a point and you win the spear. At the end of both tests, we'll tally the scores. Whoever has the most points gets to pick a prize from the luxury chest and have lunch with me."

"Who wants to go first?" Henry asked. "Cynthia?"

She selected a spear. "Do we get a practice throw?"

"No, but you get six tries."

She held the narrow pole in her hand and took aim. The spear missed the target by three feet. Cade was impressed. That was closer than he thought she'd get with her bandaged hands. He wondered if she worked out. Firm bodies like hers didn't happen by accident. She tried again. Another near miss. Again and again. Her fifth spear hit the target and bounced off. Her sixth and final toss hit and the spear stuck.

Cade clapped. "Good job."

She shrugged. "They're heavier than they look."

"Thanks for the warning." Cade threw a spear and hit the target dead center. Henry removed the spear.

"Impressive," she said.

"Just wait." Cade tossed the second spear and hit the target. As Henry removed that spear, Cade couldn't wait to throw the next. He scored with the third, but the fourth missed. By the end of the spear throwing he had four points. Sterling one.

Lines creased her forehead. "I only have one point."

"Don't worry about it," Cade said.

"Easy for you to say."

True. He felt confident and unbeatable. Not that he was competing against Sterling. Just the idea was as ridiculous as Henry in his pith helmet. "We have five spears. All we need are the snorkel and fins, and we'll be set."

Sterling nodded, but seemed more focused on the bow Henry held. No matter. Cade was the one who would win and pick the prize.

"Now for part two of the competition." Henry handed them each a bow and quiver of arrows. "Same rules apply except you'll shoot arrows at the target."

"Cade can go first this time," Sterling said.

"Thanks." He stepped to the line. "I'll show you how it's done."

She batted her eyelashes. "Oh, yes. Please do."

He felt like the king of the jungle. *Me, Tarzan, you, Jane.* His sister would laugh at him, but Cade liked playing the role of protector and hero. When he was a little boy, Grandfather Armstrong had nicknamed him the white knight. Too bad it hadn't been Robin Hood. Sterling would make a nice Maid Marion.

Cade hadn't shot a bow in years, but it was like riding a bike. He pulled back and released the tail. The arrow arced upward for ten feet and nose-dived into the sand. "Darn."

"Try again," she said. "You'll get it."

He appreciated her encouragement, but not one of his six arrows came close to the target. So much for self-confidence and being a knight in shining armor. He walked away from the line. Poor Sterling. She didn't stand a chance. "It's harder than it looks."

"Thanks for the warning." She studied the bow, took aim with a make-believe arrow and snapped the line. She looked cute pretending to know what she was doing.

"Are you ready?" Henry asked.

She aimed, released the arrow with a twang and hit the target dead center. She did the same five more times. "I win."

Cade stared at her. "How..."

She shrugged. "We were required to participate in a sport at boarding school. I didn't want to run—too sweaty—or do cartwheels—too girly—or play with a ball—too many broken nails—so I chose archery. Never thought I'd use it again. Just like calculus. Who knew?"

Henry removed his helmet and scratched his head. "I never knew that."

"You don't know everything about me."

That piece of knowledge brought relief to Cade. More relief than it should—or that he cared to admit.

She stared at the luxury chest. "Can I pick my prize now?"

Cade took a step forward. "I want to consult—"

"She won." Henry placed a hand on his shoulder. "Let her choose."

Sterling raised the lid of the wooden chest and dug around. Cade had told her what they needed—the snorkel and fins. She wouldn't choose something else.

The longer she took, the more anxious he felt. Come on, Sterling. Use that pretty head of yours. Fins and snorkel.

She rose and held a small black zippered pouch in her hands. "This is what I want."

"But the snorkel—"

"Enjoy, darling." Henry's voice contained a hint of laughter. "You earned it."

Her prize had better be something good, but Cade couldn't imagine anything good being so small. "What is it?"

"A manicure set with nail polish." Pride filled her voice. "It's not the color I would have chosen for myself, but it will do. I can give you a pedicure to thank you for my new shoes."

Cade wanted to spear himself. A manicure set was worthless. As were nail polish and pedicures. What had she been thinking?

She hadn't. That was the problem.

He felt as if he'd been sucker punched. After she got the foundation the island and the yacht, Cade had thought they were on the same team. He'd seen some admirable qualities in her, but he'd been mistaken. She was clearly a flake.

And that's when it hit him.

Sterling wasn't a nightmare as he'd originally thought when he met her at Henry's party. Bad dreams went away when you opened your eyes. But his eyes were open and she was still here holding that dam—dang little manicure set in her bandaged hands. And she would be here with him for the next two weeks and there wasn't a damn thing he could do about it.

As Cynthia lay next to Cade in the lean-to, she worried about him. He'd barely spoken today. No good nights, not even a congratulations for her archery victory. She received a grunt when she thanked him for dinner—another plate of fish, beans and rice with fruit for dessert, but that was it.

This was so unlike the Cade she'd known since arriving

on the island. But she still had a lot to learn about him. He wasn't simply a good catch; he was a decent, hard-working man.

Snores filled the air. At least Cade was asleep.

Maybe he wasn't feeling well. He'd taken more pills. Cynthia guessed his headaches were stress related. He was a bit high-strung. He needed to loosen up and put his lawyering behind him. That gave her an idea. A brilliant idea. She would make life on the island so much better for Cade that his headaches and stress would vanish. Forever.

Whatever else was wrong, she would fix that, too. She couldn't rely on looks to win his love so she would try something else. She wasn't patient enough to wait until they were off the island. She'd realized that after he'd given her the pair of flip-flops.

And Cade would thank her for everything she did. His gratitude would be the first step to something more meaningful.

Like marriage.

The next morning Cynthia woke up at the first ray of sunlight. She couldn't remember the last time she'd been up this early. The chilly air brought goose bumps to her arms, but thc tcmperature would warm soon enough.

Today was the first day of her plan to make Cade's life less stressful and win his heart. She had eleven days, including today, to make him see he couldn't live without her.

Cynthia lit the fire and spooned coffee into a pot. She guessed the amount to add. A little too strong or too weak wouldn't matter. The thought counted more than taste when one was trying to be useful, and she was going to be so useful Cade wouldn't know what to do without her help. Without her.

Her hands didn't hurt as much, and she wove her hair into two braids. Next, she washed her face. After three rinses, she still felt dirty. She stared at the jumble of tubes, tins and pencils in her makeup bag and settled on charcoal eyeliner and a mauve lipstick. Nothing else would survive in the heat, but at least her face wasn't totally naked.

Cade's snores drifted out of the lean-to. The noise hadn't bothered her last night. Maybe after twenty-five years, his snores would annoy her. She couldn't wait to find out.

Time for breakfast. The way to a man's heart was through his stomach, or so she'd heard. Cynthia wanted to fix Cade a mouthwatering, home-cooked meal. Her parents' cook, Gabby, prepared all the food or Cynthia ate out, but how hard could cooking be? A little of this, a pinch of that, and, voilà, breakfast.

The smell of smoke woke Cade. Burning, rancid. He opened his eyes and forced his tired legs to move. As he jumped out of the lean-to, Sterling dumped a bucket of water over the smoking fire pit.

She fanned the smoke away with a towel. "Sorry about the smell. It'll go away."

"We'll be home by then." He noticed the pile of burned food and charred remains. "What..."

Two empty cans of tomatoes lay on the ground. Damn. Empty wrappers and the rice container lay near the cans. Dammit. He took a step toward the can and kicked something—the empty tin of caviar. That was his bait.

"Sterling." His tone sounded harsh even to him. He didn't care. "What the hell did you do?"

"I was making you breakfast. Only you didn't wake

up so I tried to keep it warm, but the food caught on fire so I put that out. It was time for brunch so I thought I'd make you something else. But that didn't work out. So I kept trying.'' She wet her lips. ''Would you like some peanut butter and crackers?''

He glanced in the crate. Only the bottle of gin, one chocolate bar, one pear, some crackers and the peanut butter remained. ''I don't believe this.''

''I'm sorry.'' She kicked sand on the smoldering fire. ''I used a lot of the food, but I was trying to make a soufflé.''

''You need eggs for a soufflé.'' His forehead throbbed. ''And an oven.''

''No wonder it didn't work.'' She sighed. ''I also made a modified version of paella, but it didn't look right.''

''Guess Betty Crocker and Julia Child won't have to worry about you taking over for them anytime soon.''

''That's not funny.''

''I wasn't trying to be funny.'' Cade's headache exploded. He rummaged through his backpack for the ibuprofen and downed two pills.

''You okay?'' she asked.

Cade didn't answer. He was afraid of what he would say and clenched his mouth tighter. He'd realized he overreacted about her choice of the manicure set. It was her prize, not his. But after this—

''You shouldn't eat those like they're candy.'' She touched his shoulder. ''Can I help?''

He jerked away. ''You've done enough.''

Hurt flashed in her eyes. ''I was only trying to—''

''Help.'' He took a deep breath to calm himself. ''It might be better if you stopped helping.''

''But I want to do my part.''

"No, you want to leave the island, but I never thought you would try to sabotage the adventure."

Two small lines formed above her nose. "Sabotage?"

"If we're forced to leave the island because of starvation, Henry will keep inviting you to his parties. No wonder he agreed to make such a large donation. He knew you'd never cut it."

"I know how much Henry's donation means to you. It's important to me, too."

"Since when?"

"Since I agreed to stay and got Henry to donate this island and his yacht to Smiling Moon." She kicked dirt on the fire until it went out. "We're in this together. You said so yourself. I knew you were tired by the way you snored so I wanted to make breakfast so you wouldn't have to cook."

"I don't snore."

She tilted her chin. "Trust me, you do."

"Well, I'm not the only one."

Her nostrils flared. "If I ever snore it's only because my sinus passages are congested."

"You must have the entire Pacific fleet up there by the way you were sawing logs last night."

"That's...that's so mean." Sterling picked up her backpack, shoved a few items inside and looped a strap over her shoulder. She grabbed a canteen and walked away.

"Where are you going?" Damn. He'd blown it. "Sterling, wait. Let's talk about this. Please?"

She stopped and turned. "I have only one thing to say."

"What's that?"

"You don't deserve me."

Chapter Seven

Sitting in the shade of a palm tree, Cynthia stared out at the water. She'd been in the same position for hours. Watching and waiting for Henry's arrival.

He isn't coming today.

The realization hit her like the waves pounding the shore. She rested her head against her knees. If only she were a tiny crab digging a hole for itself on the beach. She wouldn't mind burying herself in the sand.

What was she going to do?

She was too worn-out and hungry to cry. She didn't want to sit here and hope Henry decided to show up. Returning to camp was her only option. But she didn't want to go back. She didn't want to see Cade. Not ever.

Footsteps sounded on the trail from the campsite. So much for never seeing him again.

"Hungry?" Cade asked.

Her stomach grumbled. No breakfast. No lunch. If only she knew what to say to him. Sorry-I-burned-all-our-food-can-you-feed-me-now wasn't going to cut it.

"I made you something special."

She didn't deserve anything special.

You don't deserve me. She couldn't believe she'd said the words out loud. Just thinking them made her cringe. Was it hot enough to spontaneously combust? That was the only way out of this. Or she could drown herself. No, she was too scared to get wet let alone put her head under water. She stared at the white-capped waves rolling to shore.

"It's a peace offering," he said.

Nice try, but she didn't know how to make peace. Yelling or fighting didn't happen at her parents' house. Making up was a foreign concept to her. She wondered if it would be cold sleeping outside tonight.

"It's got chocolate."

For chocolate she would consider a truce, surrender, peace, whatever it took. She glanced up. Cade handed her a pear half-drizzled with melted chocolate. Her stomach didn't care whether she and Cade had argued or not. It only wanted food and the pear looked wonderful. One bite wouldn't hurt. Juice dripped down her chin. She wiped it away. Okay, this was the best thing she'd tasted in days. Maybe she would take one more bite to be polite.

"Thank you," Cynthia said once she'd finished. Making up was fun and filling. "That was delicious."

"I'm sorry."

His apology caught her off guard. She expected a little more chitchat first, some witty repartee, a few confessions and admissions of flaws. But Cynthia recovered quickly. "Me, too."

He sat next to her and his thigh brushed hers. She hated the way her pulse quickened at the accidental contact.

"I know you were only trying to make me breakfast

and not sabotage the adventure, but when I saw the ruined food I lost it.''

She waited for him to say something else. He didn't. Must be her turn. ''I should have realized I was wasting too much food and stopped. We have a long way to go and it's going to be harder without our food supply.''

His eyes widened. ''You aren't leaving?''

''Of course I'm not leaving.'' Staring into his eyes, Cynthia didn't like what she saw. No trust. No future. Nothing. ''You still don't believe I'm going to stay, do you?''

''I...no.''

''I gave you my word.''

He brushed his hand through his hair. ''Some people never follow through with what they say.''

She stiffened. ''I'm not some people.''

A corner of his mouth lifted. ''No, you're not.''

''We're teammates. You said so yourself.''

''True.'' The other corner of his mouth curved up. ''But I'm used to being on a team of one so this is new to me.''

''I don't understand.'' His words puzzled her. ''Don't the Armstrongs do everything together? All for one, one for all?''

''Yes, but I cut my ties to that side of my family.''

''W-what do you mean?''

''The only Armstrongs I have a relationship with are my mother and sister.'' He stared at the horizon with a faraway look in his eyes. ''I have nothing to do with the others. Or anything else related to them, including my trust fund.''

How could he turn away from his money...from his family? Emotion clogged Cynthia's throat. ''W-why?''

''Money,'' he admitted. ''My life used to revolve

around money. I was a divorce attorney who had lost sight of everything but the bottom line. I was sucked into the Armstrong model of success. It was all about winning and losing even when it came to child custody. I'd forgotten the most important lesson I'd learned when my parents split up—nobody wins in a divorce."

"No biggie." Her voice sounded shrill. She didn't care. "You get a new job and everything's better."

"I got a new job. I founded Smiling Moon."

So he had a job. This wasn't so bad.

"I love my job, but the pay sucks." He laughed. "Nothing like being poor and having to budget to teach you how to live life to its fullest."

This wasn't happening. Cade didn't want to be an Armstrong. He didn't have any money. He wouldn't be able to provide her with the big family and the security she needed. Yet, she was still attracted to him, and that frightened her. She never wanted to be this swept away by a man. By a poor man. Her chest tightened. She couldn't breathe.

"You okay?" he asked.

No, she wasn't okay. All her dreams had been flushed down the toilet. Or would have been if they had toilets out here. She breathed deeply until her heart stopped pounding.

"You're pale," Cade said.

She was a lot of things at the moment. Pale, upset, disappointed, dejected. She slumped against the palm tree. She admired his dedication and determination to make Smiling Moon a success, but that wasn't the lifestyle she wanted. She couldn't live that way. She couldn't be poor. Not ever again. Not even for Cade.

She closed her eyes as memories assaulted her.

"Are you sure you're okay?" he asked again.

Cade aroused old fears and uncertainties. She breathed slowly and deeply. Anything to keep her from hyperventilating. ''I was remembering a time when we didn't have enough money to have a budget.''

''You?''

She nodded. ''We lost our estate and lived with friends until they got tired of us.'' She didn't tell him about skipping meals if no one invited them over or having to leave her private school and enroll in a public one. ''At one point we were homeless and lived in our car. It was the only time I heard my parents fight. My grandfather finally agreed to help us.''

She remembered the strange combination of relief and regret when her grandfather took them to their new house. The fear and uncertainty were over, but she'd hoped the love and concern her parents had shown her would continue. It hadn't.

Talk about a Catch-22. Poor and loved. Rich and unloved. Why couldn't there be a third option? Rich and loved.

Cynthia never wanted to worry about money, about feeling safe and secure. She never wanted to put her children through that kind of uncertainty, through that kind of fear. ''I will never go through that again.''

''Some people don't have a choice.''

But she did and that made her situation with Cadc clear. She might be attracted to him, but those feelings could never lead to anything. They could never be permanent.

Life on the island just got a whole lot easier. She didn't have to worry about Cade falling in love with her. She didn't have to worry about him period. They had no future together. Only the following ten days.

For the first time in her life, what she looked like, what she did or what she said didn't matter. She'd never had such freedom before. This *would* work out. And when she got back to civilization, she would call Travis Drummond. He was nice and comfortable and crazy about her. And she liked him even if he didn't make her tingle. Yes, Travis would do nicely.

Cade nudged her. "By the way, you don't really snore."

"I know." She smiled back. "But you really do."

The next day, Henry was still a no-show. When he failed to show up again the next morning, Cade radioed the ship only to learn Henry would be by later that day and was giving them time to get to know each other. And that's what they'd been doing. Except something strange was happening to Sterling. She'd lost her obsession with her looks, with her hair and with her fingernails. She'd also stopped trying to please him. Right before his eyes she was changing. It was dam—dang attractive.

She held up a coconut. "Check this bad boy out."

"Nice one." Cade gave her the thumbs-up sign. "Told you we wouldn't starve."

"Grapefruit, mangoes, coconut, fish and coffee." Sterling tossed the coconut into a bucket. "Wonder if we could hit the bestseller lists with an island adventure diet book? We could donate the proceeds to Smiling Moon."

In her tankini and braided hair, she looked like Sterling, but she sure hadn't been acting like her. She'd gone from sexy socialite to camp buddy. No primping, no flirting, no suggestive glances, a little more complaining and a lot more speaking her mind. She'd been trying hard and working harder. She even took charge of a few duties around the camp, just not cooking.

Life on the island was fun now.

Maybe being deserted on the island since Henry had

stopped showing up to play his games had changed things. Maybe the lack of shower facilities no longer seemed awful. Or maybe Sterling was showing her true self. Cade hoped for the latter.

She tossed a grapefruit in the air and caught it. "I never thought I'd say this, but our camp is growing on me."

"A home away from home?"

"It's sort of my first home," she admitted. "I live in Connecticut with my parents."

"You seem more like the city type."

"I have a pied-à-terre in Manhattan where I stay when friends like Henry are in town, but I prefer to be at my parents'. They aren't around much so if I didn't stay there I'd see them even less."

"Does your father's job require travel?" Cade picked up a coconut.

"No, he's retired, but my parents like taking vacations." She placed the grapefruit in the bucket. "They act like they're on their honeymoon when they've been married thirty years."

"Thirty years?"

Nodding, she pushed a strand of hair back into her braid.

"My parents have a dozen former spouses between them," Cade said. "They wouldn't recognize true love if it bit them in the a—er, rear."

She laughed. "But they love you and your sister, right?"

"Yes, they love us." Cade tightened his grip on the coconut he'd found. "But sometimes that isn't enough. My parents tried to stay together for Kelsey and me, but the fighting got worse. So did the cheating. When the custody hearing began, my father brought up a few of my mother's lovers. She was worried she would lose us so she hid us with distant relatives. No one knew where we were. My father was frantic so he agreed to whatever she wanted.''

Her brow knotted. ''Where were you?''

''On a horse farm in Kentucky.'' He remembered getting out of the rental car and holding Kelsey's hand. He'd been so scared. His mother couldn't stop shaking. ''We couldn't go to school so we were taught at home. It was awful at first, but became fun. In the mornings we'd help with the horses, do schoolwork and go back out with the horses. Neither of us wanted to go back to Chicago when my parents came for us. The farm was quiet with lots of work so we never got bored. We were surrounded by the land, animals and lots of love.''

''I'd love to live in a place like that.''

The sincere tone of Sterling's voice coupled with the longing in her eyes surprised Cade. She didn't seem like the hearth and home type. ''You think you could live—''

A boat horn sounded. Henry waved and waded to shore.

''The king returns,'' Cade muttered.

''More like playboy prince.'' She dusted off her hands. ''What was he thinking when he got dressed this morning?''

Henry wore a loud Hawaiian shirt with matching shorts. The bright orange and yellow matched the brilliance of the tropical sun. Leave it to Henry Davenport to make a fashion statement wherever he went. ''Maybe he's color blind,'' Cade said.

''Maybe he's finally decided to live in that Fantasyland world of his full-time.''

''Good morning, my castaways.'' Henry said as he stepped off the boat onto the shore. ''Have you enjoyed your time alone?''

''It's been okay,'' she answered.

Henry furrowed his brows. ''Just okay?''

She nodded.

''What have you been doing? How are you getting along?'' The questions spewed from Henry's mouth faster than lottery tickets when the jackpot hit a hundred million.

Cade went first. ''We're out of food and hungry.''

''There's no place to bathe and we're dirty,'' she added.

''You're the only one who's dirty.'' He rolled his eyes. ''If you would go into the water, you could get clean.''

She frowned. ''You can't take a bath in salt water.''

This had been an on-going disagreement for the past forty-eight hours. ''You can't take one in a bucket, either.''

Henry stepped between them. ''Let's not worry about personal hygiene. You both look healthy. Cynthia, you have some color.''

''It's probably just dirt,'' she said.

''It's...never mind.'' Henry rubbed his palms together. ''We're going to have fun today.''

His definition of fun left a lot to be desired. But so long as the game didn't involve eating slime, Cade was up for anything. He'd even give undressing a wet Sterling another try. ''What's on the agenda today?''

''The two of you are going on a scavenger hunt.''

Cade unrolled a scroll. Written in calligraphy on old-fashioned sepia-toned paper was a list.

''If you find all the items and return to camp by sunset, you win a special prize.''

''What is it?'' she asked.

''An inflatable bed,'' Henry answered.

No more hard floor. No more cricks in the neck or sore

lower backs. Sterling's gaze met Cade's. She had to be thinking what he was. They would win no matter what.

"Oh, I almost forgot." Henry's eyes gleamed with mischief. "If you don't find all the items on the list, I get to take something from your camp. And I choose what it is."

She frowned. "That's not fair."

"It's my game. It doesn't have to be fair, only fun." Henry grinned like a kid in a toy store. "I'll wait at your camp."

"Don't touch anything," Cade ordered.

Henry's mouth twisted wryly. "I wouldn't dream of it."

"Do you trust him?" She whispered to Cade.

"No." He helped her on with her backpack. "Let's hurry."

The clock was ticking.

"Come on," Cade urged. The sun was lower in the sky and they had one item left on the list. "We don't have much time."

"We're not going to lose." As she walked behind him, she strung flowers together. One of the scavenger list items was a lei made with fresh flowers. "But it's hard to do this and walk at the same time."

"Women are supposed to be experts at multitasking."

"We are, but this is different."

It sure was. Henry's scavenger hunt was nothing more than a mixed bag of creativity and dumb luck. Cade had never seen such a ridiculous list of items in this life—a fresh flower lei, a mango, a wood carving, a coconut cup, a sand crab, a Lokelani rose and a woven basket to hold the items in.

Sterling had woven a basket from palm leaves—like

braiding hair—and had figured out a way to make a lei from hibiscus blossoms and dental floss—a little like stringing cranberries and popcorn for the Christmas tree.

Cade didn't care about the hows or whys of what she did, but he was impressed by her creativity. He couldn't have done this without her. This game had taken their full cooperation and working together. Teamwork.

As they hiked to the interior of the island in search of a rose, Cade stared at the greenery. Lush, dense and wet. The elevation changed and the path narrowed making the hike more demanding. Sterling dragged behind. He glanced back at her pink flip-flops. She needed sturdier shoes.

"Hurry up," he said.

"It's all done." She placed the lei around her neck. "Now all we need to find is the Lokelani rose."

While she caught up to him, he studied the map printed beneath the list. "It's a little farther."

"How does Henry know this is where the rose grows?"

"Maybe he brought in his own bush and marked the location on the map. I wouldn't put anything past him at this point."

Walking at his side, she peered over. "How much time—"

A twig snapped. Something whooshed above them. As Cade dropped the map and grabbed Sterling, a net surrounded them and catapulted them into the air. She screamed.

"It's going to be okay," he said.

"How can you say that?"

They swung at least fifteen feet above the ground. She had a good point.

"Do you think Henry did this?" she asked.

"Why else would a net be in the middle of the path he had marked on the map." Cade massaged his temples.

"Another headache."

"Yes, but this one has a name—Henry."

"I can't believe he did this." Disappointment filled her voice, and once again Cade wanted to comfort her. At least now that they were "teammates" the urge made more sense.

"I know he's your friend, but I can believe he did it."

"I don't care if he's my friend," she admitted. "When we get out of here, we're sending Henry on his own adventure."

"Sounds good," Cade said. "But I'm not giving up yet."

He hadn't liked losing when he was a divorce attorney; he didn't like it now. Cade pulled on the net. As his weight shifted, the net swung back and forth.

"Stop," she cried. "We're going to fall."

"We're not going to fall." At least he hoped they wouldn't fall.

"The net is digging into my skin." Her voice sounded tight as if she were in pain, and Cade's shoulders tensed. "It hurts."

He glanced at her leg. The spot where the net pressed into her thigh was red. "If only I had my knife…."

He'd left his pack with all the items in the woven basket at the trailhead to the interior island path.

She shifted slightly. Her arm brushed his hip. "Sorry."

"What are you doing?" he asked.

"I have an idea." Her breasts pressed against him.

Remember, this is Sterling. That didn't help stop his body from reacting to her closeness. Hell-o, she was practically on top of him. Another few seconds of this and he was going to have something that would embarrass both of them. He tried to think of her as one of the guys. She was his camping buddy. His sit around the fire with, pal. His pillow pal.

That thought stopped him. She wasn't his pillow pal. They didn't have a pillow to share. Only a cramped little shelter she called home, but he'd rather be there than here. She kept squirming. The blood rushed where he didn't want it to go. "Sterling—"

"I can almost reach it." She arched against him. He was going to explode. "Just a little farther."

No kidding. Talk about torture. If he didn't know better, he would think she'd planned this. Heck, he would have set the trap himself if it meant having her crawl over and against him like this.

This might be Sterling, but the new Sterling. The one he liked, the one he couldn't deny his growing attraction to. Nothing would ever happen, but he could enjoy the ride.

"I've got it," she said finally.

"Got what?"

"My manicure set. Good thing I had it in my knapsack."

It was like getting hit with a bucket of ice water and for the best since he wanted to shove her manicure set... He took a deep breath. "This isn't the time to do your nails."

"I'm not *doing* my nails." The zipper opened. "I'm cutting us out of the net."

"With what? A nail clipper?"

"A toenail clipper," she said. "I don't think the cuticle cutter or the nail file will work."

Cade groaned.

The sound of clips filled the air. "Trust me."

He had no choice but to trust her. The minutes ticked

by. The sun was going down. Henry would win. Cade wondered what he would take—a pot, the blanket, the radio?

He tried to see what she was doing. The net swung back and forth again.

She sighed. "Stop moving."

Not even a please. Sterling had stopped trying to make him like her. Cade missed that. He'd been strangely flattered by it. But now he was confused. Friendship should have clarified their relationship, but if anything the line had blurred. He felt himself fighting his growing affection for her.

"Done," she said.

He turned without upsetting the balance. She'd cut a line through the netting. Not on the bottom where they could fall through, but on the side, where they could climb out and drop to the ground. "Way to go."

"Do you want to go first or should I?" she asked.

"I'll go first so I can catch you."

"I could catch you."

Nothing Sterling did would surprise him now. He should have given her more credit. "I'm sure you could, but we're a team. It's my turn."

He climbed out. Helping her down, he ignored how she was soft and curvy in all the right places. But having his hands on her brought back memories of their first night on the island. Memories, Cade realized, he didn't want to forget.

She zipped up her manicure set and placed it in her backpack. "Much more useful than fins and a snorkel."

"Yes, and I'll paint your nails to make up for all my wisecracks."

"I'm going to hold you to that." She put on her backpack. "We have one more item left."

Cade glanced at the horizon. ''We're out of time.''

''I'd still like to get it.''

Once again Sterling had surprised him. ''Let's do it.''

By the time they found the Lokelani rose in a vase sitting on a large rock and returned to camp, Henry was gone and he'd taken their only blanket.

''An air mattress would have been nice.''

''At least we have each other,'' Cade said.

''Yes, we do.'' She tossed branches into the fire pit. ''Are you ready to paint my nails or do you want to wait until after dinner?''

Chapter Eight

The night was chilly without the blanket, and Cynthia fought the urge to use Cade's body for warmth. Finally she gave in and lay against him, but kept her hands to herself. Cuddling appealed to her but she survived the night without touching him any more than was necessary. And that kept her going. Only seven days left. She could make it. She would make it.

If only she wasn't so dirty.

Standing on the beach, Cynthia stared at the waves rolling in. Small, not scary. The hot sand burned the bottoms of her feet, and she took a step toward the water. She needed a bath. No, she really needed a thirty-minute steaming shower with a shampoo and hot oil treatment for her hair followed by a facial and massage, but a bath or something resembling one would have to do. She took another step. That wasn't hard.

A wave broke against the shore. No way. She couldn't go in. She took a step back. So much for being brave.

Cynthia scratched her head. Maybe she could ask Cade to help wash her hair. He'd done a great job on her nails. Talk about a perfectionist. He really was sweet.

And nice and handsome and intelligent and funny and…

Poor.

Still, she liked him. Not as a boyfriend, but a friend. Cade was caring and funny and a good cook. He was also far from perfect. He was a bit of a stuffed shirt; something she found hard to believe since he rarely wore a shirt out here. His intensity surprised her. He got too many headaches, couldn't control his swearing and was too particular about roasting coconut to a specific shade of golden brown. Though she had to admit it tasted delicious when he got it right. Still Cynthia couldn't imagine being on this island with anyone else.

If only there was a shower…

Another wave hit the beach, and she backed away.

"Afraid of a little wave?" Cade asked.

Cynthia froze. She was and always had been a coward. "The water's cold."

"It's as warm as a bathtub."

She'd said the first words that had popped into her head. Weren't oceans cold? It had been so long she couldn't remember.

"Don't tell me, you only bathe in bubbling Jacuzzi tubs."

She took another step back. "Okay, I won't tell you."

"You said you wanted to get clean." He tossed a bottle in the air. "I have shampoo."

Now that was tempting. She took a step forward. A wave rolled in. Forget it. She'd rather be dirty, grimy and smelly than face the raging waters of the Pacific. "You can't wash in salt water."

"Salty is better than greasy or grimy."

"I—I can't."

"Can't or won't?" Cade swung her into his arms.

"Stop." As he waded into the water, she kicked. "Please, Cade." Panic slivered down her spine. "Don't do this. I can't—"

He dumped her into the water. She hit the bottom with a thud. A wave crashed over her and tossed her like a rag doll. Her eyes stung. She gasped for air. Salt water filled her mouth.

She was going to die.

But not without a fight.

She kicked her feet and flailed her arms. Nothing happened. She wasn't about to give up.

But she couldn't breathe. She needed air and—

"What the hell are you doing?" Cade held her upright.

"I can't swim."

His jaw tensed. "Why didn't you tell me?"

"I tried to tell you."

Waves crashed against them. She clung to Cade, burying her face against his chest. She soaked up his strength, but she was still scared. She knew how powerful and deadly a wave could be.

"You're trembling." His voice softened to a whisper.

"When I was eight I got caught in a riptide and dragged out to sea. A lifeguard saved me." She took a breath to calm her rising nerves. "I haven't been in the water since."

He pulled her closer. "I'm sorry, Sterling."

"I forgive you." She tightened her grip on him. "Can we go back to shore please?"

"Yes, but you're standing in the water."

"I—I—I am?" Cynthia didn't know whether to be proud or scared to death. She was a little of both. "I am."

''Why don't you wash off?'' he suggested.

''I don't think so.''

He gave her an encouraging smile. ''I'll be right here.''

Cynthia wanted—needed—him to keep her safe. She licked the salt from her lip. ''Can you swim?''

''Can I swim?'' Cade grinned. ''I'm a certified life-guard.''

She looked at the water again. The waves were small, rolling to shore instead of crashing. Still…

''I won't let anything happen to you, Sterling.'' With his finger he raised her chin. ''I promise.''

He sounded so genuine, but she remembered what was at stake. ''If something happens to me, you don't get the donation.''

''If something happened to you, I wouldn't care about the donation.'' A vein in his neck twitched. He seemed… serious and that made her feel better, safer. ''We're friends, Sterling. I care about you. I don't want you to be afraid anymore.''

His words comforted Cynthia, but she felt a strange twinge of regret at them only being friends. They wouldn't—couldn't—be anything more. Yet she couldn't deny her attraction to him or her respect for him. She'd never met a man like him and doubted if she ever would again. ''Thanks.''

Cade released her. ''It's okay.'' As she reached for him, he backed away. ''Try it on your own.''

The water came to her knees. It wasn't so bad, just slightly worse than a root canal.

''Let's go deeper,'' he suggested.

''Let's not.''

''Come on.'' He laced his fingers with hers, and she held on as if it were her only lifeline. ''I'll wash your hair.''

That was too good an offer to pass up. Especially since she knew he would be there for her—Cynthia's stable rock in the ever-moving water. She trusted him. Nothing would happen to her with Cade around.

''But you need to loosen your death grip on my hand.''

''Sorry.'' She took one step, then another. ''I'm doing it.''

''Yes, you are.'' He tried to release her hand, but she wouldn't let him. Cade was her lifeline, her life preserver, her life at the moment. ''A little bit farther.''

The water came to her belly button. ''No more.''

He waved the bottle of shampoo in his hand. She waded deeper until the water hit her rib cage. ''This is far enough.''

''You're doing great.''

''I don't feel so great.''

He placed his hand on her shoulder. His strong fingers kneaded her tight muscles. ''Relax and lean your head back into the water.''

She tensed more. ''I don't want my hair washed.''

''That's the funniest thing you've said all morning.'' He laughed, and she felt a tiny bit better. He had a great laugh. ''It'll be okay.''

''You're not going to let go of me and let me float away?'' Cynthia remembered her father letting go of her hand and walking toward her mother as the wave receded. It had happened so fast. One minute she'd been playing, the next she'd been dragged out to sea, alone.

''Trust me,'' Cade said.

Her gaze met his. ''I do.''

He supported her so she floated. Gently he wet her hair. The water lapped around her, yet Cade was unmovable. She wasn't going anywhere. He wouldn't let her.

''Is this so bad?'' he asked.

"No." She forced the word from her dry throat. Any other woman would be closing her eyes and moaning thanks to the pleasurable sensation of having Cade rubbing her hair and scalp. But she wasn't there yet. Life wasn't fair.

"Here comes the shampoo," he said. "Close your eyes."

She did. This wasn't so bad. As the sun's rays kissed her cheeks and the warm water surrounded her, she pretended she lay in a bathtub big yenough for two.

Cade's hands worked through the tangles and knots in her hair until he could brush his fingertips through the strands. His touch electrified. A dangerous thing while submerged in water. Perhaps the salt acted as a ground. To tell the truth, Cynthia didn't care. With each stroke of his fingers, she drifted deeper and deeper into a dreamlike state. His strong hands were so gentle. His soft touch a contradiction to the solid man she knew him to be. He kept her safe and secure.

This was how she longed to feel every day of her life. She never expected to find pure joy in the Pacific Ocean. And with Cade.

He massaged her scalp, his touch stronger, but as soothing. "Almost finished."

Cynthia didn't want this to end. Not ever.

He used the lather to wash her arms. "Okay?"

She murmured yes. He washed her legs and feet and rinsed the soap off. He did the same with the rest of her.

His intimate touch embarrassed her, but another part enjoyed it. And why shouldn't she? A gorgeous man was washing her and keeping her safe. Heat pulsed through her veins. Thank goodness they couldn't be anything other than friends or this could get complicated.

He rinsed the soap from her hair, keeping the water out of her eyes. "All done."

She stood and nearly fell over. She was light-headed and weak-kneed, but in a good way. "Thanks."

The single word seemed an inadequate gesture of gratitude, but she couldn't think of anything else to say. She tried to tell herself this is what friends do for one another, but she couldn't imagine her and Henry in this situation. She leaned her head back and pushed her wet hair off her face.

"Feel better?" Cade asked.

"Much." She glanced up and saw him staring at her. The look in his eyes made her feel vibrant and sexy. A shiver raced down her spine. Cold? The water was too warm. The air, too. No, this was something...different. Her pulse quickened.

She parted her lips to speak, but he lowered his mouth to hers before she could say a word. When his lips touched hers, a jolt of energy shot through her.

Talk about a good kiss. Better than good. Great. He made her feel beautiful, cherished, safe. His hands around her waist, he pulled her closer. Cynthia went eagerly. She leaned into Cade, soaking up the taste and feel of him. Salt, moisture, heat.

This kiss was so much more than she ever imagined a kiss could be. She opened her mouth wider, wanting more. Still that wasn't enough. It would never be enough.

His lips moved over hers, taking all she had to offer. She gave gladly, willingly. He could have whatever he wanted. Today, tomorrow, always.

Her heart pounded against her chest, against him. She almost couldn't believe this was real. But she was touching him, and the whiskers on his face scratched her skin. The kiss was real. Cade was real.

He was everything she didn't want, but it didn't matter. Not when she was in his arms, drowning in his kiss. She should care, but she didn't. Not one bit. She wanted more of him; she wanted all of him. He deepened the kiss and she went with him without any hesitation.

His kiss intoxicated. Uh-oh. She couldn't afford to become addicted to him or his kisses. Cynthia pulled away.

Thankfully, Cade held onto her or she would have fallen into the water. Her world had shifted on its axis. She'd never been kissed so completely before and that rattled her. She struggled to calm her breathing, pulse and heart rate.

"How do you feel now?"

Speechless. Worried. Overcome. Amazed.

Safe.

The strange combination left her confused and in awe of Cade Waters. Her senses seemed heightened. She felt the sand between her toes and beneath her feet. She heard the cry of a bird overhead and the splash of a wave.

Cade smiled as if he'd been unaffected by the kiss. She knew that wasn't possible. "We'll see how you feel tomorrow," he said.

Her heart leapt with anticipation. "What's tomorrow?"

Cade's smile crinkled the corners of his eyes. "That's when I teach you to swim."

Two days later, Henry showed up in a pair of shorts and a T-shirt silk-screened to look like a tuxedo jacket and bowtie, but the seriousness etched on his face ruined the fun outfit. The adventure must be wearing on him, too.

Cynthia looked forward to the end. Yes, she'd started learning to swim, had discovered muscles she never knew she had and could build a fire with her eyes closed. She also couldn't stop thinking about Cade. About the kiss they'd shared after he washed her hair. About the way both of them acted as if nothing had happened between them.

But it had.

And she wanted him to kiss her again. Maybe Henry's presence would diffuse the situation. Make her see everything clearly again. But right now all she could see was Cade. That was bad. She imagined being like her mother, so wrapped up in a man, in Cade, her own child didn't matter. She couldn't let that happen.

"During today's game, you will compete as individuals," Henry said. "Only one of you will win."

"Great." Cynthia was relieved because they worked too well together. She wanted to distance herself from Cade. This would be her first step.

Henry's brows slanted in a frown. "You're not going to argue?"

"Isn't the point of your games to compete?" she asked. "Against nature, against you, against each other?"

"You set the rules, Henry," Cade added. "We follow them."

Henry started to speak then stopped himself. He didn't look like his carefree self. Cynthia was worried. She didn't appreciate what he'd done to her and Cade with this adventure, but Henry was still her closest friend. "What's wrong?"

"Nothing I can't fix." Henry narrowed his eyes. "The winner of today's game will receive a night of luxury complete with a tent and a real bed topped by a feather mattress—"

"Down?" she asked.

"Only the finest goose feathers, darling."

She imagined herself sinking into its softness. Her back

would go into shock after all the nights on the uncomfortable bamboo floor.

''What else?'' Even Cade looked intrigued, which surprised her. He liked roughing it and was growing a beard. He'd claimed there was no reason to shave out here. She, on the other hand, would kill for a wax job.

''A fresh-water heated shower, dinner and breakfast.'' For the first time in days, Henry had their full attention. ''Champagne and wine included.''

This was so much better than anything in Henry's luxury chest. Cynthia wet her lips. ''Mimosas in the morning?''

''That can be arranged.''

Cade's mouth tightened. ''What do we have to do?''

''Race around the island,'' Henry said.

Her heart sank. ''I can't run faster than Cade.''

''Speed is only one element of this race, darling. How well you navigate the course will determine the winner.'' Henry opened his duffel bag and handed each of them a handheld electronic device. ''Waypoints have been loaded into these global positioning satellite devices. You must follow them or you will get lost. If you get lost, you will lose.''

Cade placed the device's strap around his neck and studied the small screen. He moved to the left and backward. ''Cool.''

Cynthia held her device. She wasn't sure what it did or how to turn it on, but the yellow was a nice color. ''What's a waypoint?''

Henry explained how the GPS, as he called it, worked and how waypoints marked the trail she needed to follow. She listened, but was still confused. She was at a disadvantage, but for a hot shower, nothing would stop her.

''Think you can do this?'' Henry asked her.

Holding on to the strap, she studied the small unit. "Yes."

"You will go in opposite directions along a circular course. Midway you will find two flags. Pick up the flag with your name on it and follow the course all the way around. The first one back with their flag wins." Henry gave them each a full bottle of water, and she smiled at his thoughtfulness. This was the Henry she knew and loved, not the one who wanted them to eat worms. "It's hot, so don't forget to drink water."

Cade assumed a race stance. If he believed this would be a cakewalk, he was wrong. She wanted to win as badly as he did. She readied herself.

"On your mark, get set, go," Henry yelled.

Cynthia ran as fast as she could. She wanted the night of luxury almost as much as she wanted another kiss from Cade.

The sweat trickling down Cade's back turned into a stream. He raced as if there were no tomorrow. He had to win. Winning would prove he wasn't going soft.

He ran toward the interior of the island where the foliage got denser and greener. Moisture dripped from the tall trees. Rain or dew? Cade didn't care. He kept going.

So what if Sterling was an amazing kisser with an incredible body, a sharp wit and a generous heart? He wasn't falling for her. She was nothing like Maggie. That alone was the biggest red flag where Sterling was concerned, but it wasn't the only one. Cade couldn't forget what was at stake. He wasn't here for fun in the sun with a beautiful woman—make that a socialite. He was here for a donation. Anything else was a complication he neither wanted nor needed.

No footpath or trail cut through the brush. Branches

scratched his arms and legs. He kept running. Cade glanced at the GPS screen and stopped. Damn, he'd missed a waypoint. He was off-course. How had that happened?

Backtracking, he got back on course. This race was about following directions, not about speed. He needed to slow down and pay more attention. Still he hurried.

Cade wanted to win so badly he could taste it. He wasn't meant to be part of a team. No room existed in his life for anything but Smiling Moon. Only the foundation hadn't occupied his thoughts in the last few days. Sterling had. This race would prove he worked better on his own. Alone. Without *her.*

He entered a clearing and saw two flags—a red one with Cynthia written on it and a blue one with Cade. He was first. Adrenaline surged through him and he pumped his fist. But he hadn't won yet. No celebration until he'd reached the finish line.

Victory wasn't a certainty. He wouldn't be surprised if Sterling won. She was a tough competitor. She'd overcome her fear of the water and started learning to swim—albeit dogpaddle—in the ocean. She could do anything she set her mind to. She was tougher, more resilient than he ever imagined and he respected her too much to count her out of this or any competition.

Stop thinking about her and stay focused.

Cade grabbed the flag and took off. He heard something in the bushes. Branches snapped. Leaves crunched. A bird or an animal? He didn't have time to be curious. It sounded big. Big enough to be trouble. Nothing was going to interfere with the race. Survival of the fittest, that's what it was all about. He kept running. Cade reached the finish line and raised his hands in the air. ''Yes, I win.''

''Congratulations.'' Henry shook Cade's hand. ''How far behind is Cynthia?''

''I don't know.''

Henry's forehead creased. ''Didn't you see her?''

''No.'' Cade realized he should have passed her on the course. He remembered the noise in the bushes. Ah, hell. Had that been Sterling, not an animal? ''I'll find her.''

''She's got the GPS.'' Henry sat. ''She can't be lost.''

Cade stared in the direction she'd gone. All his senses went on alert. He listened for any sounds. Nothing. ''She could be hurt.''

''She'd scream if she were hurt.'' Henry motioned to his portable DVD player. ''Want to watch a movie?''

He sounded so nonchalant. Cade didn't get it. Sterling was stronger than she looked, but she still wasn't used to being in the outdoors, in the wild. ''She could be in trouble.''

''Cynthia will be fine.'' Henry sipped from a soda can. ''It's hot out here.''

One worst-case scenario after another had Cade moving toward the course. ''I'm going back—''

''She'll be here soon.''

Maybe, but what if she wasn't? Cade couldn't wait around for her to show up. That was irresponsible. Wrong. They were teammates. Partners. Friends. ''I'm going—''

''Hi.'' Sterling carried her flag. He didn't see her water bottle. Her cheeks were flushed, her clothes drenched with sweat. She frowned when she saw him. ''I lost?''

''Sorry, darling.'' Henry packed up his bag. ''Cade won.''

She plopped onto the ground with a loud sigh. Cade noticed her raw knees. Scratches covered her legs. A narrow stream of red ran down her right calf.

Blood. Sterling's blood.

His vision blurred. Cade clutched Henry's chair. He had to pull himself together for Sterling.

"I can't believe I lost," she said.

Cade was more concerned with her injuries. Funny, but he didn't feel as squeamish as he thought he would seeing her cuts and scratches. "What happened to your knees?"

"I stumbled and dropped the GPS. I had to crawl into a bush to find it. I should have put the strap around my neck." She extended her dirty arm. "Congratulations, Cade."

He shook her hand. "You okay?"

Before she could answer, Henry rose. "Let's go."

Cade held onto her hand and didn't want to let go. "Are you going to be okay by yourself?"

"I'll be fine," she said without any hesitation.

He released her hand, picked up his backpack and took a step toward Henry. Cade wanted this; he'd won fair and square, but he couldn't enjoy a night of luxury knowing Sterling was here alone. He turned to her. "You go instead."

Her mouth dropped open. "But you won."

It didn't make sense to him, either. He admitted to himself that he was a little attracted to her. Okay, a lot. "I know how much you want a shower."

He hoped that didn't sound as stupid to her as it did to him.

Anticipation twinkled in her eyes. "You'd really do that?"

"Is that allowed?" Cade asked Henry.

"By all means." Henry grinned. "If that's what you want."

Cade nodded. "I want her to go in my place."

"Thank you." She threw her arms around him. Her

body pressed against his, and her warm breath caressed his neck. She brushed her lips across his mouth. "Thank you so much."

No, thank you. He wasn't sure which he liked more—her impromptu kiss or the hug. If only he could have another one of each to decide the winner. But that wasn't possible.

A swim to bring his body temperature back to normal and another meal of fruit and fish were all he was getting tonight. But fish would help lower his cholesterol and fruit was good for him. And Sterling was happy. That was the most important point, one he didn't want to examine too closely.

Falling for her? Okay, maybe. "Have fun."

"I will," she said. "But I don't mind staying here."

Cade knew she meant it. His admiration and respect for her grew exponentially. "Go."

Waving goodbye, he noticed a smug expression on Henry's face. Cade didn't have time to ponder it, though. He wanted to grab a swim and start a fire before the sun went down.

"Wait," Henry said.

Cade stopped and turned.

"Since Cade has so unselfishly relinquished his night of luxury, I will allow both of you to come with me." Henry's eyes sparkled with mischief, and Cade knew not to put anything past his wealthy host. "But I must warn you, there's only one bed."

"That's okay," she said. "Isn't it, Cade?"

All he could do was nod. He couldn't stop thinking about her hug and her kiss. Sharing a bed wouldn't be easy. Hell, it would be impossible. Sharing the lean-to had been bad enough. With no blanket, they only had clothing and each other for warmth. He wouldn't call sleeping side-by-side cuddling. They'd touched only to keep warm. It had been a necessity, one that had caused him sleepless nights for the past few nights. If not for an afternoon nap each day, Cade would be running on fumes. No way could he share a real bed with Sterling unless they were going to do a lot more than sleep.

Every one of his muscles tensed.

"You're coming, aren't you?" Henry asked.

A mixture of unsettling emotions ran through him. He might be confused, but Cade wasn't stupid. "I'm coming."

Chapter Nine

The sun had just faded beneath the horizon, yet an evening of luxury had never been finer or more appreciated.

Cade showered, shaved and put on a white linen shirt and drawstring pants he found hanging on a hook in the bath cabana. For the first time in nine days, he felt clean. He walked to the dining cabana unable to believe Henry had transformed this portion of the island into such a luxurious getaway. Three white tents had been erected on the beach. One for showering, another for dining, a third for sleeping.

The setting was something out of a movie. Very romantic. His wedding-coordinator sister, Kelsey, would love the setup. Very newlywed. A canopy covered with sheer fabrics and tulle housed the dinner table. Garlands of tropical flowers draped over the chairs and hung from the canopy. A candelabrum with crystals dangling from each of the four arms provided a romantic glow. Classical strains of a string quartet played from a boom box and set the elegant mood. The scent of the sea mingled with the fragrance of exotic flowers, but neither made his mouth water or his stomach growl like the food prepared by the yacht's chef.

"Hello." Sterling wore a sleeveless white linen dress. "You clean up nicely."

"So do you." Cade pulled out a chair and she sat at the linen covered table. He took a seat across from her.

She handed him a flute of champagne and raised her own glass. Shadows from the candlelight flickered on her face, accentuating her high cheekbones and full lips. "To Cade Waters."

He appreciated her not using his middle name. "I don't deserve a toast."

"I strongly disagree." The gold flecks in her eyes danced. "You were unselfish to offer me this night of luxury. The least I can do is offer a toast and raise my glass to you."

A kiss would be nice, too.

He didn't know where the errant thought had come from. Some deep dark place in his subconscious? He wished. No, her kisses were at the forefront of his mind. And the brush of her lips this afternoon had only whetted his appetite.

Her glass tapped his. As the perfectly pitched chime carried in the air, he took a sip of the bubbly.

Champagne, music, candlelight.

No wonder he'd thought about a kiss from Sterling. The romantic atmosphere demanded kissing.

And it hit him. This place. The adventure.

Henry was setting them up. Everything made sense. The games, having them get to know each other, tonight. Leave it to Henry Davenport to play Cupid. Cade sipped his champagne. Two people couldn't be less suited for each other than he and Sterling. When she found out…

No, Cade couldn't tell her.

Her friendship with Henry had already been damaged. Nothing was going to happen romance wise so she didn't need to know about Henry's matchmaking attempt.

She lowered her glass from her lips. No lipstick marred the rim of her crystal flute. She hadn't put on makeup after her shower. She didn't need any.

His gaze lingered on her oh-so-perfect-and-kissable mouth.

Cade almost laughed. He was paying too close attention to what she did and didn't do. Bet Henry would be pleased. But romance was not a possibility. No matter how beautiful she looked tonight.

"What's so funny?" she asked.

He'd been caught with his hand in the cookie jar. Might as well confess. "Just thinking."

"About?"

"You," he admitted. "You're beautiful."

"Thanks." She ran her fingertip up the stem of her crystal flute. "But I bet you say that to all the women you're marooned with on a deserted island."

"Can't pull anything over on you, can I?"

She smiled. Sterling had a great smile and mouth and lips. Lips made for kissing. Dam—darn, he was back to that again. Not that it surprised him. He'd been thinking strange thoughts about her these past two days. Only two days, a little voice teased.

"Ready?" she asked.

For a kiss? He focused on her eyes. "For what?"

"Dinner." She removed the cover from one of the platters. "I'm starving."

As she served the food, he opened a bottle of Chardonnay and filled their wineglasses. They ate in silence. Marinated chicken, rice pilaf, lightly buttered asparagus and French bread. The food was filling and delicious and exactly what they needed.

She leaned back in her chair. "I can't eat another bite."

"Don't forget the fresh fruit and cheese platter and a dessert tray."

"I'll skip the fruit, but if there's any chocolate..." She sighed. "Don't you wish every night could be like this?"

Cade sipped his wine. "Tonight's been nice, but it would get old after awhile."

"It would never get old to me." She studied him over a chocolate brownie. "Don't you ever miss what you gave up?"

He thought back to his life before Smiling Moon. "Honestly? No. I was a different person then. Parties, clubs, traveling, work. Lots of work. But it didn't make me a better person. I was tired and hung over and...a real jerk," he admitted. "I was only interested in making more money and getting the best settlement for my clients."

"What changed?"

Maggie. He took a sip of his wine. But not even her canceling their wedding and walking out on him had made him see the truth. No, it had taken something else.

Emotions battled within him. Regret, guilt, betrayal. "I was involved in the divorce of a friend, Thad Riley."

"Riley Wear?"

Cade nodded. "He married his college girlfriend, Jenny, after she got pregnant, but he wasn't ready to settle down. Not even after they had two more children. Jenny got tired of his cheating. He wouldn't go to counseling so she filed for divorce. Thad wanted full custody of the three kids though he'd said prior to the separation that Jenny was a wonderful mother.

"I put together a case to prove this wonderful stay-at-home mom was unfit and got Thad temporary custody. Two weeks before our court date, I received a phone call. One of the kids was in the hospital. Thad had been having sex with the nanny and the kids wandered outside. Little Max rode his tricycle into the street and got hit by a car.''

As Sterling leaned over the table, her eyes darkened with concern. ''What happened to Max?''

Cade remembered arriving at the hospital and seeing the look of shame on Thad's face and the look of hatred on Jenny's. ''Max was seriously injured, but recovered. It could have been a lot worse.''

''What his poor mother must have gone through and you...'' Sterling's understanding gaze met his. ''You couldn't let Thad have the kids.''

''I couldn't. A harsh, but necessary wake-up call.'' Cade swirled the wine around in his glass. ''Thad didn't want the kids as much as he didn't want Jenny to have them. He also didn't want to have to pay child support on top of alimony.''

''What happened?''

''I wouldn't represent him. My boss forced the issue. I quit. As a child advocate, I saw so many at-risk kids. The problems they faced... I realized divorce wasn't the worst thing that could happen in a family. I wanted to help these kids. Not with pro bono work or when it was convenient, but all the time. So I started Smiling Moon. The rest is history.'' He picked up the wine bottle. ''More wine?''

''Any more wine and I'll fall asleep right here.''

Cade smiled. ''Go ahead. I'll sleep in the bed.''

''It's big enough for two.'' Sterling glanced at her empty plate and bit her bottom lip. ''I mean, we share the lean-to and have had no problem. We're just friends, right?''

"Right," he answered, a little too quickly. But a bed in a beach paradise was a far cry from the shelter they called home. And after kissing her... "You can have the bed, I'll put the feather bed on the ground and sleep there."

"Take the bed," she said. "I don't mind the floor."

"We'll flip for it."

"I don't have a coin."

He thought for a moment. "Rock, scissors, paper?"

She nodded.

Time after time they tied.

"This is ridiculous," Cade said finally. "We're both adults. We've been sharing the lean-to. That's no different."

"No different at all." She didn't sound so confident. "It's just a b-bed."

Still they lingered over dessert and coffee and aperitifs. Sterling's eyelids looked so heavy she could barely keep them open.

"Tired?" he asked.

She nodded. "You?"

"Exhausted."

"Good, we'll both sleep." Her cheeks reddened. "I mean—"

"I know what you mean." And he did. If they were both tired, they would lie down, close their eyes and fall asleep. Nothing to worry about, nothing else to think about. Sleep was all that would happen. He prayed that was true.

Cynthia entered the tent and inhaled the sweet scent of roses filling the air. An old-fashioned lantern illuminated the interior. The fabric walls shimmered, softening the sound of the ocean outside. She felt as if she'd been transported to another place, another time.

As she walked toward the bed, her bare feet sank into a plush throw rug. She saw the bed and froze. White rose petals covered the queen-size bed and the fluffy pillows.

The bed was more luxurious than anything she could have imagined, more romantic, too. This wasn't a bed meant for sleeping. Her heart lodged itself in her throat.

"Wow," Cade said.

Wow summed it up, but hardly did justice to the night's sleeping quarters. Lush, elegant, romantic. Honeymoon worthy.

Cynthia took a deep breath and exhaled slowly.

"Do you want to change into something more comfortable?" Cade asked. He wore the shirt and pants he'd found in the cabana.

She didn't have any other clean clothes besides a swimsuit she'd rinsed out in the shower. And that wouldn't do. She wanted—needed—as much fabric between them as possible. "The dress is fine."

"What side do you want?"

At home she slept in the middle of the bed with one of her parents' cats on either side of her. "Doesn't matter."

"I prefer the right." Cade crawled into the bed without clearing any of the rose petals. Tired, or in a hurry? Her pulse quickened. He snuggled deeper into the soft pillow. "This has to be the most comfortable bed in the history of the world."

"We've been sleeping on bamboo poles." She cleared the petals off her pillow. "A piece of plywood would be an improvement."

He grinned. "You'll see."

She climbed into bed and sunk into the down featherbed. It was like sleeping on a cloud. "Oh, my."

"Told you so."

"Yes, you did." She snuggled deeper into the bed and pulled the soft cotton sheet over her. "I lay corrected."

The lantern flickered shadows over the fabric panels ruffling in the sea breeze. It didn't seem real. She had no idea how Henry had pulled any of this off and she didn't care. Tonight she wanted to live the fantasy.

"I'm going to turn down the light," Cade announced.

She pulled the sheet up to her neck. "Okay."

The tent went dark.

"Quite a night," Cade said.

No date, no anything would ever come close. The only thing missing was a good night kiss. But inside this romantic canopy, in this bed meant for lovers, it wasn't going to happen. The last thing she wanted was to be involved in a carbon copy of her parents' relationship. "Thank you for sharing it with me."

"You're welcome."

The sounds of the night filled the air. Waves crashed against the shore. Leaves bristled in the breeze. Cicadas chirped. She wanted to say so many things to Cade, but the words wouldn't come. She wanted to touch him, but the space between them seemed as insurmountable as Mt. Everest. He was everything she didn't want, yet that didn't matter tonight. What about tomorrow and the day after that? She couldn't be sure.

And she had to be sure. About everything.

Maybe she would dream about Travis instead of Cade. She could only hope. "Good night, Cade."

"'Night Sterling."

Sunlight filtered through the canopy's sheer fabric. Cade opened his eyes feeling rested. He never thought he'd fall asleep with Sterling next to him. But he had.

The bed was comfortable. Cozy and warm. He brushed his hand through his…wait a minute that wasn't his hair. And those long blond strands covering his chest weren't his either.

Sterling.

She curled against him, her head on his shoulder. It had felt so natural, so right, he hadn't noticed. That surprised—no, shocked—him. He'd never liked waking up with Maggie draped all over him. He'd had a king-size bed and that had seemed too small, but with Sterling…

It was so nice, comfortable, soothing.

Cade didn't want to wake her. He watched her sleep. Her eyelashes shadowed her cheeks. Her serene smile suggested a pleasant dream—a day at a spa, a shopping spree, a vacation at a five-star resort. Anywhere but this island. He wondered if she dreamed of him. Of the kiss they'd shared in the water. Of other kisses and touches and…

She shifted. Her eyes blinked opened. "Cade?"

"Good morning." He smiled at her tousled hair and wrinkled dress. She looked cuddly and adorable. Two adjectives he never thought she would be when they first met. "Sleep well?"

"Yes, but…" She glanced around the tent, tossed off the sheet and sat. "It's morning?"

Her dress had inched up to her panties. The polite thing to do was look away, but he was transfixed by the curve of her hip.

As a blush crept across her cheeks, she tugged on her dress and pulled the hem lower. She stared at the foot of the bed.

He struggled for the right words to say. It wasn't every

morning he woke with a gorgeous blonde snuggled next to him, legs entwined, hair spread across his chest. Just thinking about her sent his temperature spiraling upward. He could get used to this. And like it. Cade blew out a puff of air.

Something was happening between them. Something disconcerting. Being friends was one thing. This was another. Luckily they had only a few more days on the island.

"Good morning," Henry called from outside the tent. "Are you sleeping in there or doing something else I can sell pictures of over the Internet?"

Leave it to Henry to have perfect timing. Or maybe it was bad timing this morning. Cade brushed his hand through his hair and said, "We'll be right out."

Sterling crawled out of the bed. "What does he think we're doing?"

Cade raised a brow and glanced back at the bed.

"Oh, oh no, he doesn't think, I mean, you and I." She stared at the bed. "That we—"

Sterling was so cute when she got flustered. "He's simply being Henry."

"Well, one of these days being Henry is going to get him into trouble and I'll get my revenge," she said.

Cade had no doubt. "Make sure I'm around to see it."

"I'm thrilled you're having so much fun in there," Henry called. "But your breakfast is getting cold."

Breakfast was the magic word. "Hungry?" Cade asked.

"I shouldn't be after last night—" She combed her fingers through her sleep rumpled hair. "—but I am."

He kissed the top of her hand and bowed. "Your mimosa awaits, milady."

* * *

Henry finished the last bite of his croissant and rose from the table. "It's time to return to your camp."

Cynthia wrapped a banana nut muffin in a napkin and placed it in her backpack. She stood and looked around. She wanted to remember every detail, flower and scent from this enchanted place and tuck the memories away in a special corner of her heart. Here in this romantic Shangri-La, she and Cade had been isolated from the adventure, from the hardships of island life.

Part of her hated to leave, but Cynthia knew it was for the best. Last night had been a fantasy—a dream. Nothing had been based in reality. Not even her feelings toward Cade.

As they hiked to the camp, Henry whistled. He was back to his old self. The unfamiliar lines creasing his forehead were gone and his smile hadn't wavered once. Maybe the stock market had gone up and he'd made another million or two.

She followed him onto an outcropping of rocks. He stopped and drank from his water bottle. She and Cade did the same.

"I almost forgot." Henry tucked his bottle into a loop on his high-tech fanny pack. "People have been calling about your whereabouts, darling."

She screwed the top onto her canteen. "Who?"

"Travis," Henry said. "He's concerned and wants to make sure you're wearing sunscreen to protect your fair skin."

A flicker of annoyance coursed through her. Cynthia knew she should be thrilled Travis took the time to call about her. But she wasn't. She knew enough to wear sunscreen. He might have meant well, but she was still annoyed.

"Who's Travis?" Cade asked.

"Travis Drummond," Henry answered much to Cynthia's surprise. "Nice guy, modest fortune. Runs his father's business. And he has a soft spot for Cynthia."

"We're just friends," she clarified. And they were. Friends, that was. Until she got off the island and away from Cade. Travis's kisses were nothing to write home about, but they were nice. Cade's brief kiss could fill an encyclopedia on emotions and physical reactions. Travis worshipped her; Cade treated her as an equal. But they weren't equals. She could easily drown in his eyes, lose herself in his kiss and forget anyone else mattered but him. No, Cade wouldn't do.

Henry drew his brows together. She didn't understand his funny look. He didn't want her to be with Travis so why should he care how she termed the relationship?

"Close friends," Henry added with a wink.

She wanted to kill him. Her relationship with Travis was none of his business. She took a step. "Let's go."

"Don't you want to know who called you from Connecticut?"

Mother and Father. Her parents must have realized she hadn't returned as scheduled. Excitement raced through Cynthia. She'd waited her entire life for this and it felt better than she imagined. She moved toward Henry and her foot slipped. She stumbled. Cade's lightning fast reaction kept her from hitting the rocks. He held onto her waist. Her backpack pressed against his chest. His warmth and his strength seeped through the fabric of her dress. She struggled for a breath. "Th-thanks."

He released her, but the heated imprint of his hands lingered on her skin. So what if she was attracted to him? Such a heavy physical attraction would only get in the way of being the best mother she could be. Yes, Travis was the better choice. No, the best choice.

She focused on Henry. "What did my parents say?"

"I'm sorry, darling." Henry's voice softened as did the look in his eyes. "Bridget called. She was frantic."

Bridget was her parents' longtime housekeeper who treated her like the daughter she'd never had. But it wasn't the same as Cynthia's parents calling. Just once she wanted them to notice...something. She was an adult, but a part of her still felt like the clumsy little girl dressed in pink, driven each week to ballet class by the chauffeur. She wanted to dance for her parents and show them how graceful she could be, but not once had they come. That hurt then. This hurt now.

"I promised Bridget you would be home in another week," Henry said. "Call her with your flight itinerary."

"I will." She sipped more water as her resolve to be a better parent than hers had been grew. She would never put her children through this. She would attend every class, every game, everything. And she'd keep track of their travels once they were out of the house.

Henry glanced at his watch. "Game time approaches."

She didn't want to play. Not when she was so torn up inside about her parents. About Cade. If only he was as comfortable as Travis. But Cade was dangerous. Cynthia feared losing herself in him. At times, she already had, and she would not have a marriage like her parents. Not unless she chose not to have kids. But she wanted the entire package—security, stability, family. Travis could give her that. Better than Cade could.

"You'll need to change into your swimsuits when we get back to camp." Henry climbed down the rocks. "And Cynthia, you might want to wear a one-piece since you'll be swimming."

She stopped. "Swimming?"

"The game involves a swimming relay and mud," Henry said.

Mud's only redeeming quality was its usage as a spa treatment, but soaking in plain old dirt and water sounded better than swimming. She bit her lip. At least she would be able to focus on something other than her parents. Or Cade.

"We ate a big breakfast," Cade said. "I'm too full to swim."

He didn't want her to have to admit she was afraid. Bubbly warmth flowed through her. Cade was such a special…friend. He's more than that, her heart cried out, but she ignored it.

"That's too bad." Henry headed through a narrow trail surrounded by lush ferns. "The prize was an inflatable mattress with bedding and two items from the luxury box."

After sleeping so comfortably last night, she didn't want to return to the bamboo floor with no blanket or pillow. "If I can wear a life vest during the relay, I'll do it."

"Yes," Henry said.

She straightened her shoulders. "We'll play."

Cade's lips tightened. "It's swimming, Sterling."

"I know." She appreciated his concern and drew strength from it. From him. "We have to do this."

"But—"

"No buts." She placed her hands on her hips. "Afraid you're not a good enough swim instructor?"

Cade laughed. "Let's do it."

Henry grinned. "Now those are the words I love to hear."

Chapter Ten

That night, Cade tossed a branch on the blazing fire. The memory of Sterling swimming to the platform and back during the relay filled him with pride. ''You were amazing.''

Sitting on a log, Sterling shrugged. ''It's not hard to dog paddle with a life vest on.''

''It was still an accomplishment.'' He sat next to her. ''And we have lots to show for our efforts.''

She laughed, the sound warm and soothing. ''I can't believe you picked a bag of marshmallows.''

He smiled. ''I can't believe you picked a tackle box.''

''We still have a few days left and I'm getting used to eating fish,'' she admitted. ''Though I was worried we were going to need pain pills, but that's no longer an issue.''

''What do you mean?'' he asked.

''You were popping pills like candy for your headaches.''

''But no longer.'' Cade couldn't remember the last time

he'd gone this long without a headache. His doctor had claimed they were stress related and prescribed a battery of tests until Cade had no choice but to believe the diagnosis.

The gold flecks in her eyes intensified and matched the colors flickering in the fire. "Island life agrees with you."

He'd assumed island life with Sterling would increase his stress. At first, it had, but now Cade enjoyed the freedom, the lack of responsibility, and the fun. "Life's simple out here."

"It is." She roasted a marshmallow. "I don't miss some of things I thought I would."

"Such as?"

"Television, shopping, high heels." She stared at her pink flip-flops. "Did you know I've never gone this long without wearing heels?"

"What about when you were a kid?"

"I wore tights and patent-leather Mary Jane's."

"A style maven even then." He popped a marshmallow into his mouth.

"Bridget said I came into the world wanting a coordinating layette to go home from the hospital in."

"Bridget's the one who called Henry about you."

"She's my parents' housekeeper."

"What's wrong?"

Sterling glanced up. "Why do you think something's wrong?"

"About a foot of your stick is on fire and your marshmallow is nothing more than a burnt offering," he explained. "You might feel better if you talk about it."

She dropped the stick. "You sound like a girl."

He grabbed another stick, stuck a marshmallow on the end and gave it to her. "I have a sister so I know the routine."

She sighed. ''I wanted a sister and a brother, a big family so there's always someone to share secrets with and open up to.''

''Open up to me.''

''Opening up might leave a hole deeper than the Grand Canyon.'' She placed her stick in the fire. ''Just kidding.''

But Sterling's voice wasn't lighthearted. And she wasn't meeting his eyes. He missed that. Cade enjoyed how she looked into his eyes, her gaze making him feel as if he were the only one in her life. On this island, he was. ''Sterling—''

''It isn't important.'' She toasted her marshmallow. ''It's rather pathetic to tell you the truth.''

His hand brushed her skin, once soft and flawless but now covered with dirt, scratches and bug bites. She turned away from him, but he wasn't going to let her do that. It was none of his business, but he wanted to know. ''Is this about Travis?''

''No.''

Her answer brought a strange relief. ''Please tell me.''

''My parents,'' she admitted. ''I thought they called about me, but it was Bridget. She's the only one who cares.''

I care. The thought came out of nowhere, and he struggled to understand it. He cared because Sterling was his teammate. That's all it was. All it could be. Ever.

''My parents wouldn't know if I was alive or dead unless Bridget told them.''

''I thought you lived with them?''

''I do.'' She removed her stick from the fire. ''If not, they might forget they have a daughter.''

''Come on.''

''I'm not kidding.'' She blew out her flaming marshmallow and stuck her stick back in the fire. ''My parents' love is something out of a fairy tale or stalker movie. They are each other's whole world.'' Sadness filled her voice. ''There isn't enough room in their world for anyone else, including me.''

Cade remembered what Henry had said about her parents. ''You're their daughter.''

''Doesn't matter. I'm still in the way. I think that's why I'm an only child. My mother said babies were much harder work than she or my father ever realized. One was more than enough.''

''Raising children isn't easy.''

''How hard can it be when nannies, housekeepers and boarding schools raise them for you?'' Sterling shrugged, but the look in her eyes was anything but indifferent. ''It shouldn't matter after all these years. At least Bridget knew I wasn't home.''

Cade didn't have an answer, but his heart ached for Sterling. So many things about her were beginning to make sense. He put his arm around her.

''Don't worry,'' she said. ''I'm not going to cry. This island adventure has toughened me up. Sorry you had to be a witness to my pity-party. I'll go get lost in the jungle now.''

''No you won't.'' He gave her hand a squeeze. ''I'm glad I'm here. That's what friends are for. We're friends, aren't we?''

''I—I…'' She tilted her chin. ''Yes, we're friends.''

''Like you and Henry?''

Two lines formed above her nose. ''Henry's like a brother.''

Cade's feelings for Sterling weren't brotherly. Not in the slightest. ''I already have a sister.''

''Good, I mean—''

''I know what you mean.''

In the depths of her eyes he saw a completely different woman than he'd seen before. A woman who longed to be loved and cherished. A woman who pretended to have more confidence than she really had. A woman he cared about. Teammate, friend, something more…

Her lips parted slightly. He shouldn't kiss her, but she needed to be kissed. He repeated those words to himself once his lips found hers. He repeated them when her mouth opened farther. And once again when he tasted her sweetness and her warmth.

This was for her. Not him.

Yeah, right.

But he wasn't listening.

He couldn't hear anything except the blood roaring through his veins and his heart thundering in his chest.

Yes, she needed him to kiss her, to let her know she was loveable. He wasn't about to let her down. So he kept kissing her and kissing her and…

What he was experiencing wasn't simply a kiss. A kiss was what they'd shared in the water. A kiss was when she'd thanked him for letting her have his night of luxury. This was something else. Something earth-shattering, rock-his-world incredible.

And it was Sterling in his arms.

Disbelief and awe ran through him. Adding those two emotions to the longing and need already pulsing through his veins incapacitated him.

Not exactly true since he was still kissing her. But that's all he was capable of doing. Kissing and breathing. He had to be breathing. Unless he'd died and this was heaven. He wouldn't be surprised because nothing had ever felt so right.

But this wasn't about him. About what he wanted. About what he needed. This was for Sterling. Forget about enjoying this more than he should. That didn't matter. She did.

Her fingers splayed his back and she arched toward him. Her breasts pressed against him. And he felt her heart beating as rapidly as his. Pulling her closer seemed natural, normal, right. That alone should have made him stop kissing her and take a step back. He didn't. He didn't want to. No, he corrected, Sterling didn't want him to.

Liar.

He ignored the truth. Ignored everything except how perfect it felt to have Sterling in his arms, his hands in her hair and his lips against hers.

He never wanted to let her go.

Desire mixed with desperation. The heady combination had him pulling her onto his lap. A moan escaped her lips. The throaty murmur sent his temperature soaring higher.

Oh, Sterling. He lost himself in her kiss, falling deeper into an abyss he never wanted to escape.

This was all he ever wanted. All he ever needed.

It's about her. Not you.

But it wasn't. Not by a long shot.

The realization made Cade draw the kiss to an end. Sterling scooted off his lap and sat next to him. Her cheeks were flushed, her lips swollen from his kiss.

How had she made him feel this way? Regret, excitement, confusion, anticipation. She was supposed to be his worst nightmare. She stood for everything he didn't believe in. Or at least she had when they began the adventure.

Now? He didn't know the answer. He shouldn't have asked the question.

She watched the roaring flames in the fire pit. The silence lengthened the short distance between them. Cade didn't know what to say, what to do. A part of him wanted to kiss her again. But he couldn't. He wasn't looking for a woman to share his life with. And even if he were, Cynthia Sterling was the last person he would choose. Yes, she had changed during the time on the island, but she still wasn't Maggie. He couldn't forget Sterling wasn't the woman of his dreams.

Yet what he felt was real. And that kiss…

Hot damn.

Glancing over at him, she looked vulnerable and shy and totally adorable. "My marshmallow is toast again."

Cade stared at the sizzling marshmallow on a hot rock. He knew exactly how it felt. He laughed. "I'll get you another."

"Thanks," she said. "And thanks for the, um, kiss. It was…"

"Amazing."

"Amazing's a pretty good description." Her eyes twinkled, and he was happy he'd said the first thing that came to his mind. "So what happens now?"

Another kiss? No. Sterling was a complication he didn't need. Making Smiling Moon a success was his priority. He couldn't make any mistakes. Nor could he afford any more kisses. Not only was his bank account empty, so was his heart. She deserved more than he was capable of giving.

"We got caught up in the moment, in the… adventure," he explained. "We should forget the kisses ever happened."

Her gaze held his, but she said nothing. He waited for her to disagree, to come up with a rationalization that made sense so he could kiss her again. She nodded instead.

"You agree?"

''I do,'' she said.

''Good.'' But saying the word felt bad, wrong and the worse move he'd made in years. ''Great.''

''Yes, great.'' She emphasized her agreement with another nod. ''Forgetting about the kisses is the smartest thing we could do. It's time to move on.''

''Exactly.'' Cade wanted to move on. So why did he feel like he'd been slapped across the face? He stared at her smile. She wasn't torn up about this, not one bit. He expected to argue his case. Present his evidence. But that hadn't been necessary. And that bothered him. Way more than it should.

Cynthia lay mere inches away from Cade on their new air mattress and bedding. The comfort level, however, didn't exceed her confusion level. With the new bedding she couldn't justify inching over to sleep against him. She hadn't liked the cold, but she loved the closeness and using his body for warmth.

And that was only the beginning of her problems. No matter how many times she closed her eyes, she couldn't fall asleep.

She couldn't put the way his lips felt against hers out of her mind. It was confusing and disconcerting, especially since she wanted to kiss him again.

The kiss in the water had merely been a teaser, a sneak preview of the upcoming summer blockbuster. And now that she'd experienced her favorite movie of all time, she wasn't going to be allowed back for a second showing.

At least she had the memory. Her lips still tingled. Her nerve endings, too. Her body craved his warmth, her skin his touch. Would memories be enough?

Cade made her feel sexy and beautiful and desirable. Three things she never thought she'd feel here on the island or even back home without her arsenal of beauty aids and closets full of designer clothes.

He challenged her to do her best and overcome her fears. She'd never felt so alive or happy with herself and the person she was becoming. Cade had played a large part in all of that.

She wanted to know everything about him. What he loved, what he hated. What he got for his tenth birthday. Most importantly, she wanted more kisses. Lots more kisses.

But it wasn't possible. She'd seen the regret in his eyes after they kissed. He didn't want any more kisses. She couldn't afford any more. The price would be too high.

Memories were all she could take with her. Kisses didn't pay bills. Tingles didn't provide financial security.

Neither of those mattered, her heart cried out.

Yes, they do, logic countered.

But logic had discounted Cade Waters, the man. Solid and strong, he made her feel safe and secure, as if she belonged in his arms and at his side. She'd never felt more complete in her life. His middle name and his family connections were meaningless. Not only to Cade, but to her, too. Money had nothing to do with her feelings.

It wasn't as if they would be destitute and homeless. She had her own trust fund, meager compared to the fortunes of Henry, the Armstrongs or even Travis, but she could keep a roof over their heads and food on the table and could pay their kids' college tuition. Okay, state university, not Ivy League, but that would be fine. What was wrong with living off *her* money?

A combination of strength and pride filled her. Until this adventure, Cynthia thought she needed a man's money to take care of her and provide for the future. She'd discounted what she was capable of bringing into a marriage. But no longer. She didn't want to be a trophy wife. She wanted to be an equal.

She could be Cade's equal.

But you could lose yourself in him. Don't forget about your children.

Cynthia hadn't forgotten about them. When Cade stopped kissing her, she'd been surprised and confused and off-kilter. But she hadn't thrown herself at him begging for more kisses. She hadn't lost herself in him, allowing desire to rule both her heart and her head. She could still see the situation logically.

And that gave her hope.

Hope for the future. A lifetime of Cade's kisses versus a lifetime of Travis's. Cynthia sighed. Maybe being comfortable wasn't the only thing she should want out of a marriage.

Eleven days on the island. Cade couldn't wait until the adventure was over. Being this close to Sterling 24-7 drove him crazy. He was afraid to sleep fearing he'd wake up with her in his arms again. But as long as he was awake, she was on his mind. Kisses and hugs. Sterling. Hugs and kisses. Sterling.

He made a final slice through a mango and grabbed another. Anything to keep busy.

Island fever. Nothing else explained what was happening to him. The new air mattress hadn't helped. Forget about being comfortable, he preferred the bamboo floor to the bed. Anything to put more space between Sterling and him. Wait. Bed and Sterling didn't belong in the same sentence. Bed equaled sex and Sterling....

Where was she? She'd gone searching for fruit, but should have been back by now. "Sterling?"

No answer.

"Come on back," he yelled. "I know you're hungry since we didn't eat breakfast. I have mangoes."

No reply. She must have found something good.

"If you're playing hard to get, it's not going to work."

Cade laughed. Her playing hard to get was working. Instead of being relieved when she agreed to no more kisses, all he could do was wonder why. He knew his own reasons; he wanted to know hers.

"Caaaaaaaaaade."

Blood roared through his veins. Every muscle tensed. Tightening his grip on his Swiss Army knife, he ran toward the sound of her scream. His arms pumped. He couldn't imagine what was wrong. They were on a deserted island. But the sound of her scream shook him to his very core. Sterling might have started out as a pain, but all that had changed. She'd changed. He liked having her around. Liked how she smiled, liked how she laughed, liked a whole lot of other things about her.

Damn Henry. If anything happened to Sterling, Cade was going to kill him.

He reached the beach and saw Sterling holding a glass bottle in her hand. She held it up. "Look what I found. There's a message inside."

Cade took a calming breath. "Why did you scream?"

"I thought it was a jellyfish." She studied him. A smile as bright as a solar flare erupted on her face. "You were worried about me."

"I wouldn't exactly say worried—"

"I would." She touched his arm. "That's so sweet."

Now he was irritated. "It's not sweet. It's business. Without you, I can't get the donation."

Something—amusement?—glimmered in her eyes. "You running so fast until you're out of breath is only about the money?"

"Donation," he corrected, trying to calm his ragged breathing. "And the answer is yes."

But it hadn't been. His only concern had been for Sterling and her safety. He hadn't thought about the donation. Not for a moment. Trouble. He was in big trouble. Cade brushed his hand through his hair.

"Let's see what the message says." She pulled a piece of paper from the bottle and unrolled it. "*X* marks the spot. It's a treasure map."

"Another one of Henry's games."

"How could he do this?"

"How has he done any of this?"

"Good point." She studied the map. "Want to see what we find?"

"Sure," Cade said. "Let's get our backpacks and canteens."

The map led them from the beach and through a grove of trees and up a steep hill. As the trail leveled, the foliage thickened leaving little room to walk on the narrow path.

She held the map. "It should be just ahead."

"I see something." Through a bush, he saw a clearing. There was a grass hut that looked as if it had come straight from Gilligan's Island, a fire pit fully stocked and a picnic basket and blanket. "Guess Henry decided to give us lunch."

"It seems too easy," she said.

Cade saw a boom box with a "push play" note on it. "Let's see what our host has in store for us today."

He hit the button.

"Good day, my castaways," Henry's voice said from the speakers. "Today you will experience village life. You will dress in traditional garb and perform traditional tasks. Inside the tent, you will find all the necessary supplies and information to prepare a traditional feast. And if you do all of this, you will be able to take the picnic basket back to camp with you. It's full of enough food to last you until the end of your adventure. And just so you don't think I can't see what you're doing, I can. Aloha."

"Big brother is watching."

"He probably has the entire island wired with cameras."

Cade thought about their kiss by the fire. Sterling's gaze met his. No doubt she was thinking the same thing. "Henry wouldn't go that far," Cade said, hoping that was true.

But he would have to be on guard. Henry wanted to play matchmaker. Cade wasn't going to do anything to make him think he was succeeding.

"We'd better get busy," he said.

A few minutes later, Sterling walked out of the hut. She looked beautiful in the grass skirt she wore over her bikini and a garland of flowers in her hair. Cade, on the other hand, hid in the bushes. No way was he coming out where anyone could see him.

"Cade?" she asked.

"Cade has been abducted by a roving band of villagers," he said through the leaves. "He won't be coming back."

She smiled. "Come out."

"No." He sounded like a three-year-old. He didn't care.

"There's lots of yummy food in the picnic basket that will be all ours if we can do this." She gasped. "There's even chocolate. Oh, please, Cade."

Cade didn't want to disappoint her. Walking toward her, he'd never felt so foolish. He wore a leather loincloth that looked like something out of a Tarzan move and ti leaves woven into ropelike wreaths around his biceps. "Don't laugh."

"I wouldn't dream of it." She sighed. "You look..."

"Stupid?"

"Sexy." She grinned. "I like it. A lot."

Sexy? Cade didn't know what to say.

"In fact, I'd better get busy chopping the fruit and making poi or I'm going to do something I might regret."

The way her eyes sparkled made his blood boil. He wanted her to have regrets. Lots of them.

"What do you have to do?" she asked.

He wished she had asked what he wanted to do instead. "Dig up the pig that's been roasting since yesterday."

Spending the day preparing a luau would never have sounded like fun to Cynthia, but it was fun. Almost like playing house. And she enjoyed it. More than she should.

But she didn't care. She and Cade would never get this chance again. For now, she would pretend it was real. She was the wife; he was the husband. Tomorrow she could go back to the adventure and the fact that no future existed between them. But until then she would pretend this was the future. Their future.

She carried wooden bowls of fresh fruit and poi to the area they'd set up for the luau. Cade had lit tiki torches. All the food smelled delicious. The fact that they had made everything themselves filled her with pride. Normally her dinner parties consisted of coordinating with her parents' cook or calling a caterer.

Once dinner was over and their stomachs were full, the stage-show began. Cade went first per Henry's instruction. Dressed in what she could only describe as a loincloth more suited to a Chippendale dancer than a villager—she'd have to thank Henry for that—Cade beat a rough-hewn drum and blew a conch shell. She applauded.

He bowed. "Your turn."

As Cynthia turned on the boom box, her heart pounded in her chest. The strains of a Polynesian song played and she danced. Tried, at least. She mimicked the movements she remembered from the hula dancers at Henry's birthday party only her hips couldn't keep up with the beat and her hands moved awkwardly. Eight years of ballet and she was as graceful as an elephant on Rollerblades. Discouraged, she glanced at Cade.

He gave her a thumbs-up. "You're doing great."

His encouragement kept her going. As she swayed her hips with the beat, the movements flowed together. Her dance wasn't perfect, but she didn't care. She focused her gaze on Cade. She'd never felt so free in all her life. Henry might be watching somehow, but this was for Cade and Cade alone. As the tempo changed, she moved toward him. "Join me."

He did.

She danced with Cade—two bodies, one rhythm. She wished the song could go on forever, but it ended much too soon. Just like the adventure would be ending soon.... She didn't want to leave the island. She didn't want to leave Cade. Not ever.

Her gaze held his. Kiss me, her eyes pleaded. Somehow he must have understood or she'd spoken her desire out loud.

Cade lowered his mouth to hers. The initial touch of his lips had always been soft and gentle. Not this time. The kiss demanded, ravished, tortured.

She didn't think any kiss could beat the one they'd shared by the fire. She was wrong. She soaked up the feel and taste of him. Sweet like the coconut drink they'd drunk with dinner, warm like the tropical night air and male like him. Cynthia didn't know if this would be their last kiss, but if it were she was going to make the most of it.

Hunger drove her. Need, too. She rose on her tiptoes and leaned into him, taking the kiss deeper and deeper until she couldn't get any closer. Her hands splayed his back, and she ran her fingertips over the ridges of muscle. He cupped her head with his hand. A moan of pleasure escaped her lips. He was everything she'd ever wanted or needed.

Lose herself in Cade? No way. She'd found herself in him.

Rain fell, the drizzle turning to a deluge. She backed away from him almost in a daze. He grabbed her hand and pulled her into the hut.

"What do we do now?" Cynthia knew what she wanted him to say, but was afraid to say it herself.

"Sleep." Cade handed her a large woven mat. "Don't forget, big brother is watching."

Cynthia had forgotten. She'd forgotten everything, but Cade and his kiss. For once that didn't scare her and she wasn't about to analyze what that meant.

Chapter Eleven

Another sleepless night for Cade. The way Sterling had danced for him with such freedom and expression had been a real turn-on. It was all he could do to keep his hands off her. If not for Henry and the possibility of cameras… Somehow Cade managed to fall asleep.

In the morning, he hiked down the wet trail littered with branches and leaves from last night's storm. "Be careful."

"Bare feet work better in the mud than my flip-flops," Sterling said. "But some of the branches are sharp."

He glanced back and watched her make her way down the steep portion of the trail. He remembered when she'd worn high heels in the sand. That day seemed like years ago, not days. Sterling had come a long way, working hard and putting her all into every job. She'd adjusted to island living and woke up each morning with a smile on her beautiful face. A lot of women would complain or nag about the lack of modern conveniences. Not her.

"Are you going to give up high heels when we get

back to civilization?'' he asked, curious if the changes would carry over once they left the island.

''You never know.'' She wet her lips. Slowly. Seductively. His groin tightened. ''Some men prefer their women barefoot.''

Cade nearly raised his hand. He would prefer Sterling anyway she wanted. No, he wouldn't. Once they left the island, he'd never see her again. He ignored the regret this realization brought.

''What do you like?'' She raised a brow. ''Bare feet or pink flip-flops?''

''Bare feet are nice, but so are the pink flip-flops.''

She rolled her eyes. ''Lawyers are good at saying a lot of words, but not really saying anything, aren't they?''

''I'll take the fifth.''

Her grin disappeared.

The look on her face squeezed his heart. ''Just kidding.''

''Oh, Cade.'' She covered her mouth with her hands. ''Our camp.''

He turned and froze. The storm had turned the camp into a disaster area. A palm tree had fallen on top of their shelter. Everything else was in shambles. ''It'll be okay.'' But even as he said the words, he knew nothing would be okay.

''It's ruined.''

The anguish in her voice tore at his heart. Everything had been destroyed except the wooden crates. At least they still had the radio.

''I can't believe our little home is gone.'' She stood in front of the splintered lean-to. ''All that work you did...''

''We did.'' Putting his arm around her, he pulled her close. ''We built the shelter together.''

''We have to rebuild it.''

"Are you up for it?" he asked.

"Yes." Renewed strength filled her voice. "Nature might have won this round but I'm not giving up yet."

He wouldn't have expected anything less from his Sterling.

Not that she was his. She wasn't. And wouldn't be.

She was simply Sterling. Someone he liked and respected. Someone he would miss once this was over with. Someone he wished he could kiss each night before he went to bed and every morning when he woke up. He picked up a palm frond. "Let's do it."

Cynthia pulled on the bamboo pole sticking out of the ground, but the piece wouldn't budge. "It's stuck."

"I'll find another one," Cade said.

She wasn't giving up. "I'll try pushing it and..."

The pole broke. Cynthia's momentum carried her forward. She stuck her hands out in front of her. Her fingertips hit the mud followed by her hands and arms. A knife-edged pain sliced through her left foot. She screamed.

Cade kneeled by her side. "What hurts?"

She moved slightly. Raw, jagged pain ricocheted through her foot and up her leg. She glanced down. The bamboo had pierced her left foot. Blood seeped from the exit wound on the top. "M-my foot, but don't look."

He didn't listen to her. One glance and he paled.

As he swayed, she reached for him. "Cade—"

"I'm fine." He closed his eyes for a moment and opened them. "I'm going to radio for help."

As Cade sprinted away, tears stung Cynthia's eyes. She didn't want to cry, not after she'd come so far. But her foot hurt so badly. She concentrated on her breathing and on Cade. He would know what to do. He would take care of her.

Cade returned and covered her with a blanket. ''Henry is on his way. He's having a chopper pick you up.''

''But the two weeks aren't up.'' Her gaze met Cade's. ''We'll lose. You'll lose.''

''You need to get to a hospital.''

Nothing but compassion and concern filled his eyes. ''But—''

''No, buts.'' He placed his fingertips on her lips. ''This isn't up for discussion.''

This wasn't the way she wanted the adventure to end. She fought to control her swirling emotions and closed her eyes. ''I'm sorry.''

''There's nothing to be sorry about.'' Cade brushed loose strands of hair off her face. ''You're so pale. Do you need anything?''

You. She didn't care whether Cade had one dollar or a million. As long as they were together… ''Everything I need is right here.''

He smiled. ''It won't be long.''

She almost laughed, but it would have hurt too much. ''We're in the middle of the South Pacific.''

''Henry told me we're on a small, private island not far from Hawaii.'' Cade wiped her face with a damp cloth. ''Henry had the captain sail around to throw us off.''

''Everything…?''

''Compliments of Henry,'' Cade explained. ''Only the storms were real.''

Real, fantasy…Cynthia wasn't sure of the difference. She felt weird, light-headed, cold. ''I want to go home.''

''You can go home soon.'' His gentle tone reassured her. ''Hang in there, okay?''

The horn from Henry's boat sounded, and relief washed

over her. Minutes later he and other members of his crew arrived.

''The helicopter will be here soon.'' Henry touched her cheek. ''You'll feel better once we get you out of here.''

She didn't want to leave. ''The adventure...Cade's reward?''

''Cade can finish out the two weeks for both of you. I won't hold your injury against either one of you.'' Henry held her hand. ''If Cade stays, you both win.''

A pain squeezed her heart. Cynthia didn't want Cade to stay on the island. She wanted him to go with her. She needed him. She...loved him.

Cade stared at her, his eyes dark. ''Do you want me to stay?''

No, she wanted to scream, but didn't. ''I...the donation?''

His gaze held hers, and she knew what he was going to do. Her heart felt as if it were breaking into a million pieces. Cynthia wasn't sure what hurt more—her foot or her heart.

''I'm staying,'' he said.

She swallowed around the sob rising in her throat. A part of her understood. She knew what Smiling Moon meant to him and how much Henry's donation would help all those kids. But another part, a bigger part, was devastated.

She might be Cade's teammate and his friend, but Smiling Moon came first. She wasn't a priority with him. It was just like her parents. Cade was just like her parents. The emptiness threatened to overwhelm her.

The whir of a helicopter filled the air. Several minutes later, a team of EMTs entered the camp. They wanted to be cautious and not remove the piece from her foot until they arrived at the hospital. They set about stabilizing her.

Cynthia had never been in so much pain. Her foot would heal, but her heart? Never. Tears welled in her eyes, but she wasn't going to cry. She'd shed too many tears in the past about her parents. She wasn't about to do the same over Cade. An EMT hooked up an IV.

"Would you like your reward now?" Henry asked.

A heaviness centered in her chest. She needed something to think about and take away the hurt. "Please."

Henry reached into his bag, pulled out a black velvet covered box and opened the lid. "Here's your reward, darling."

A sapphire and diamond necklace and matching bracelet glistened in the sunlight. Henry had remembered how much she loved the set when they'd seen it during one of his trips to New York.

As she touched the precious jewels, tears clouded her eyes. She loved the jewelry, but had hoped to have her fiancé or husband give it to her. Her heart wished Cade had been the one to give it to her, but she appreciated Henry's generosity. "Thank you."

"You earned them," Henry said.

Yes, Cynthia had. And she was proud of her accomplishment. "Where's the matching ring?"

"Greedy, aren't we?" Henry grinned. "Someone else is going to have to buy you the matching ring."

It wouldn't be Cade. The realization tore at her. No matter, she could buy the ring for herself.

"Would you like me to put the necklace on you?" Henry asked.

"Please."

Cade took the necklace. "I'll do it."

He moved her braid and clasped the jeweled necklace around her neck. The gesture was bittersweet. Her sense of loss went beyond tears. The bamboo pole was finally freed from the ground.

Cade straightened the teardrop-shaped diamond in the center. "It's perfect for you."

No, you're perfect for me. Cynthia took a deep breath, and then another.

"We need to go," one of the EMTs said.

Staring at Cade, she didn't know what to say. Goodbye didn't seem enough.

He kissed her forehead. "Take care, Sterling."

"You, too, Armstrong." She wasn't sure where the name came from. At this point, she didn't care.

One edge of his mouth tilted up. He didn't seem upset at her lapse. "Make Henry pay," Cade whispered.

"I will."

"Goodbye."

She didn't think her heart could break any more, but it did. "Bye."

She waited for him to say he'd call, but he didn't. He handed her backpack to Henry.

Cade helped carry the stretcher to the helicopter and stood back as she was loaded inside. Henry climbed in after her.

Cynthia waved to Cade. He waved back. The door slid closed. That was it. The adventure and her time with Cade were over. She closed her eyes.

Henry smoothed her hair. "It's going to be okay, darling."

No, it wasn't. Nothing would ever be okay again.

As the helicopter rose from the beach, Cade shielded his eyes from the blasting sand. As the whir of the rotors faded, a sinking feeling settled in the pit of his stomach.

Sterling.

Her "Bye" had been an uppercut to his chin. He'd been flattened, knocked out, down for the count. And he was just catching his breath and standing up again.

All he could see was the sadness in her eyes when he'd said he was staying. Cade didn't know why she cared. They didn't have a chance together. They wanted different things out of life. He could never make her happy.

Rich woman, poor man. Their relationship would be like his parents or the reverse of his situation with Maggie. Poor woman, rich man. Either way love would fall victim to money. He and Sterling would end up like his parents—miserable and divorced and fighting over who got what. Or like Maggie—struggling and arguing over what a prenuptial agreement meant in the grand scheme of a marriage.

Henry's adventure was ending the best way possible.

So why did Cade feel as if he'd made the wrong decision?

Smiling Moon needed Henry's donation to succeed. Cade had no other choice but to remain on the island and finish out the adventure. He'd made the right decision.

But he missed Sterling already. He missed her smile, her laughter, her.

What had he done?

She'd wanted him to come with her. And he hadn't.

Regret stabbed his heart. He'd rationalized his decision with the donation. But that was a bunch of bull.

It was all about money, about winning, about making Smiling Moon a success.

Darn. No, damn. Cade plopped on the sand.

No matter how many times he told himself he'd changed, he hadn't. He was the same as he'd always been—an Armstrong through and through. He'd justified his actions because Smiling Moon was a charity. But he was as driven to succeed with his nonprofit foundation as he'd been with his law practice. Everything still boiled down to money and success.

Maggie had realized the truth even after he walked away from his family, his fortune, his job, everything. That's why she'd stayed with her then boyfriend-now husband. She'd seen what Cade couldn't—he wasn't going to change. He cradled his head in his hands.

Maggie.

He'd loved her once and she'd become his ideal. But he'd been wrong about everything he'd done these past five years. About Maggie, about Smiling Moon, about himself. He'd gone to the extreme with all his decisions. There had to be a happy medium somewhere.

Cade stared at the horizon.

What he wanted now was so clear. He wanted Sterling. She wasn't the ideal he'd dreamed about, but she was real.

Cade loved her.

But he'd hurt her.

You should have gone with her.

No kidding. He'd made the worst mistake of his life. Once again he'd put money before love. But it was worse than that. Cade knew how her parents treated her, yet he'd acted the same. He'd given her no reason to believe he loved her.

But he would convince her of his love and ask for her forgiveness. Beg, if necessary. He wasn't about to lose her.

Cade ran to the camp, grabbed the radio and called the ship. No answer. Only static. And then he remembered Henry had gone with Sterling.

Dammit.

As Cade fiddled with the radio dials looking for a channel, he prayed for an answer. Someone had to be out there, someone who could take him to Sterling.

What a wonderful dream. Cynthia lay in a field of flowers. The most wonderful scent—a luscious fragrance of every imaginable blossom—surrounded her. She didn't want to wake up, but her pain medication was wearing off.

She opened her eyes and realized she hadn't been dreaming. Her hospital room overflowed with bouquets of flowers and potted plants. Tropical flowers, long-stemmed roses, orchids and carnations. The gesture had Henry written all over it.

The door opened and a copper-haired nurse dressed in white peered into the room. "There's a good-looking guy who's been waiting to see you. Are you up for company?"

Cade. He'd come for her. Cynthia's heart leapt. She combed her fingers through her hair and adjusted the blankets on her bed. "Yes, please."

Travis Drummond walked into the room with a huge bouquet of red roses. "Hello, Cynthia."

It wasn't Cade. She blinked the tears from her eyes and straightened her shoulders. "Thanks for stopping by."

"I've been here since last night," Travis approached her bed. "They wouldn't let me see you right after the surgery."

Circles darkened his eyes and his clothes were wrinkled. She wet her dry lips. "You've been here all this time?"

He nodded. "I've been so worried about you, Cynthia. I've been worried ever since you left for the island. When I heard about the accident… Did Waters do this to you?"

"No, it was my fault."

All of it was her fault. Her foot. Her broken heart.

"Don't worry. Everything will be fine." He stroked her hair. His large hands seemed almost clumsy now, but she knew he meant well. "Once you're released, we can go to the Grand Wailea Resort on Maui. The Grande Spa will do wonders for you. They do massages on the beach. You won't have to lift one of your beautiful fingers. You can recuperate and get back to normal."

"Normal?" She wasn't sure what normal was anymore.

"You can have your hair done. A massage. Facial. All those things women love."

Those were the things she loved. Why didn't that make her feel better?

Travis smiled. "I'll take care of everything."

But she liked taking care of things herself. She wasn't a porcelain doll to be left on the shelf so she didn't get cracked. She could build a fire, make a mean pot of coffee, find coconuts and weave a basket from leaves.

"Until Henry's party, I didn't believe in love at first sight." Travis stared at her with adoration in his eyes. "I missed you, Cynthia. I want us to spend time together. Lots of time."

She'd always hoped to find a man to say those words to her. Yet she didn't feel as good as she thought she would.

"I believe we could have a future together." He held her hand. "A happy future."

Before the adventure she would have sold her soul to have a man like Travis say those words to her. She would have declared victory for his concern. She would have packed her bags for the resort while dialing a wedding consultant at the same time.

Would have.

Those were the key words.

She'd changed, and she liked the changes. Oh, she still preferred a hot shower to bathing in the ocean, wished her roots weren't starting to show and needed to have her legs waxed. But those things didn't determine who she was or what she wanted out of life.

She preferred being Sterling, not Cynthia.

Cynthia wanted comfortable. Sterling wanted love. Travis would make her the center of his world and give her anything she desired. She saw it in his eyes when he looked at her, heard it in his voice when he spoke her name. But she didn't love him. Not the way a wife should love a husband. He deserved more. So did she.

Everything made so much sense. Love didn't have to be exclusive and hurtful. Love was a choice, one her parents chose not to include her in. But she would love differently. Her love would include children, friends, so many others.

"Travis..." She didn't want to hurt him, but she had to be honest. "I appreciate all you've done. All you want to do..."

A muscle at his jaw twitched. "I hear a 'but' coming."

"But I'm not the same woman I was before I went to the island. What I thought I wanted before isn't what I want now."

"Meaning me?"

"Meaning a lot of things," she admitted.

"I could fall in love with the new you."

"I need to get used to the new me first," she said.

"And then?"

Hope filled his eyes, but she couldn't lead him on. "I honestly don't know."

"Does this have anything to do with Waters?" At her nod, Travis sighed. "Thanks for telling me the truth."

The door swung open, and Henry rushed in. ''I spoke to the nurse who said you had company and… Oh, it's you, Drummond.''

''Hello, Henry. And goodbye. I was just on my way out.'' Travis kissed her cheek. ''Good luck, Cynthia.''

She sighed. She didn't need luck. She needed a miracle.

Chapter Twelve

As the door swung closed, Henry sat in the chair next to the bed. "How do you feel?"

A void had taken the place of her heart and she had a hole in her foot. Other than that... "I've been better."

"Your doctors say you'll recover fully." He brushed her hair off her face. "Plastic surgery will help the scar, and with physical therapy, you won't limp."

She didn't care about a scar or a limp, but Henry did. She forced the corners of her mouth up. "That's good news. Thanks."

He looked at the flowers, at the window, at her foot. "I only wanted to make you happy, but I messed everything up. I'm sorry, darling."

"It was an accident."

His gaze met hers. She'd never seen him so upset. "I'm not talking about your foot."

"I'd do it again. All of it." Even fall in love with Cade. Her heart tightened. "Things didn't work out as I hoped, but I learned a lot about myself during the adventure. I wouldn't trade that opportunity for anything. In spite of a bum left foot."

Henry studied her. "You've come a long way, Cynthia."

"I have." And she was proud of that.

He held her hand. "What can I do to make things better?"

Her feelings were too raw to discuss so therapy was out of the question. "The flowers are lovely."

"Please don't tell me I shouldn't have."

"I won't. Because you should have." Her smile was real this time. "And I'd love a chocolate milkshake."

"Anything else?"

Cade. But not even Henry could manage that. "There's a matching ring to the necklace and bracelet I won."

"I'll see what I can do." Laughter returned to Henry's eyes. "And I'll call your parents."

If Henry called, would her parents come? For once it didn't matter. "Don't call them."

"But you're all alone."

"I'm not alone." She squeezed his hand. "I have you."

The waves tossed the fishing boat back and forth like a dingy. The smell alone would make the sturdiest of fishermen sick, but Cade was holding it together.

Thank goodness he'd reached this small fishing boat with the radio. The father and son who operated it had gone out of their way to pick him up and make him comfortable. But they couldn't take him where he needed to go.

Desperate for sleep, he struggled to keep his eyes open. Once he found a quicker way to reach Sterling he could nap, but not until then. He'd wasted enough time waiting for this boat to pick him up from the island. He couldn't waste any more.

Gripping the satellite phone, he listened to the ring on the other end and thanked the wonders of telecommunication technology. He remembered the telephone number to his uncle's direct line, but Cade hadn't used it in years. Had the number changed? Would anyone answer? Would Uncle Alan speak with him?

"Alan Armstrong's office," Vanessa Phillips, Cade's uncle's long-time assistant answered. "How may I help you?"

"It's Cade."

Silence. He thought she might have dropped the receiver.

"How are you, Cade?" Vanessa asked. "It's been what? Two, three years since you've called?"

"Five." He struggled to keep his voice steady when it wanted to crack from the strain of the past. "Is my uncle available?"

"He's always available for you," Vanessa said to Cade's surprise and relief. "One moment, please."

Cade waited. Each passing second brought to mind one more way he'd failed. His heart hammered in his chest.

What if Uncle Alan wanted nothing to do with him? Cade had been the one to walk away from the family, blaming his failed relationship with Maggie on the prenuptial agreement required by his trust fund. Cade had been the one to accuse his uncle of being a modern day Scrooge after he took Cade's access away from his money when he wanted to turn over the trust fund to Smiling Moon. No, Cade wouldn't blame his uncle for not talking to him.

"It's so good to hear from you, Cade." Concern filled

his uncle's voice as he answered the phone. "Are you okay?"

"Not really." Admitting the truth was easier than Cade thought it would be, but he'd never been this desperate before. "I didn't know who else to call, Uncle Alan."

"I'm happy you chose me," Alan said. "I've missed you, Cade. We've all missed you."

Emotion clogged his throat. He couldn't speak.

"Tell me what you need," Alan said the way Cade hoped he would. "Whatever it is, you've got it."

He took a deep breath. "I'm on a fishing boat somewhere off the coast of Hawaii. I need to be picked up and taken to shore as fast as possible."

Cynthia was dreaming again. Only this time the smell of raw fish overwhelmed the scent of the flowers. Raw fish? Blinking open her eyes, she saw flowers and...Cade. He sat on a chair by the window looking ragged with dark circles under his eyes and whisker stubble on his face. His clothes were wrinkled and stained. The fish odor emanated from him.

His presence confused her. Maybe she was still dreaming or had an extra dose of pain medication. No, her foot hurt too much for it to be that. Must be real. "Wh-what are you doing here?"

He rose from the chair, walked to the bed and handed her a small black case. "You forgot your manicure set. I figured you might need it."

"You're here to return my manicure set?" She wasn't buying it. "What about the donation?"

He shrugged. "Easy come, easy go."

"Nice try," she said. "Tell me the truth."

His brow creased. "After you tell me how you are feeling."

"Tired, sore, hungry."

"Not much different from the island except you have a bed." He patted the mattress. "And you're clean. I could use a bath."

"You aren't wearing a new cologne—Mahimahi-male?" His smile annoyed her though she had made the joke. "Why are you here, Cade?"

"I wanted to see you."

"You're seeing me." Part of her was happy to see him. The other part was angry at him for not leaving the island with her. She hated the way she wanted him to touch her, even kiss her. Her feelings made no sense. Hadn't she learned her lesson with her parents? Cade was no different. She straightened her shoulders. "How did you get off the island?"

"It's a long story."

She motioned to her foot. "I'm not going anywhere."

He explained about using the radio to contact a small fishing boat and then transferring to a larger vessel that brought him to shore. Too much effort when the adventure would have been over in just another day.

"You shouldn't have gone to so much trouble."

"You're worth the trouble."

"Me?"

"I should have gone with you."

Her mouth went dry. She struggled to understand. "But the donation for Smiling Moon—"

"Isn't as important as you are." He kissed the top of her hand, the one without the IV. "Staying on the island was the biggest mistake of my life. After what happened with Maggie. After I left my job. After I founded Smiling Moon. So many afters… I thought I'd changed, but I hadn't changed. I pretended not to be an Armstrong who focused on success and money, but that's who I was. Am. I didn't realize the truth until you left.

"For the past five years I've taken everything to the extreme. I blamed being an Armstrong on my parents' divorce and my own shortcomings and walked away from my family when I needed them most. I believed I couldn't be happy without Maggie. I was wrong.

"You've made me a better person, Sterling. You loosened me up, helped me enjoy myself and have fun. You took my headaches away and showed me life isn't black and white. All or nothing. Shades of gray are okay, too."

As she stared at him, all of her anger vanished and her heart filled with love. She basked in the knowledge she had done as much for him as he had for her. Cynthia realized they had a chance together. She wasn't sure what the future held, but that was okay. The journey was as important as the end result.

"Say something," Cade said. "Say yes."

"Yes?"

"Yes, you'll marry me."

As he reached for her hand, Cynthia's heart slammed against her chest and she struggled to breathe.

"Okay, proposing marriage is crazy. We haven't known each other long and the short time we have known each other has been like a roller-coaster ride. When I first met you I didn't like you, but on the island I got to know you. Not the dressed-to-the-nines socialite named Cynthia who does and says all the 'right' things, but the woman beneath the perfect makeup and hair. The real you. Sterling. The woman who blistered her hands and conquered her fear of water and listened to me talk about Smiling Moon and my dreams and who shared her own dreams of marriage and a family with me.

"I can't offer you a lot of money or a big house in the

country or a summer place on the beach. But I can love you. And I do love you, Sterling. I'll always love you."

"But Maggie—"

"Isn't the one for me. I loved her once, but those feelings don't come close to the love I have for you. You're not perfect, but neither am I. Together we make a darn good team. I know we'd make a great couple and even better parents.

"Tell me I still have a chance." The heartrending tenderness of his gaze tugged at her heart. "Tell me I haven't lost you forever."

Tears of happiness welled in Cynthia's eyes. His words filled her with more love than she thought possible. The only thing she wanted was Cade. Money, clothes, a nice house. None of those things mattered as much as love. "You haven't."

"I felt so lost when you left the island. When I realized what I'd done, I physically ached. I was desperate for you, desperate for your love. I had to make it right, but I knew I couldn't do it alone. I contacted my uncle, Alan Armstrong, and asked for his help. He arranged for another ship to pick me up."

Cynthia knew what a big step this had been for Cade. She didn't think it was possible, but her heart swelled with more love for him.

He smiled. "By the way, he's arriving tomorrow. He wants to meet the woman who brought me back to the family."

More tears filled her eyes. "I'm so happy for you."

"Be happy for us." From his pocket, Cade pulled out a small black velvet box and opened the lid. A diamond surrounded by sapphires glimmered. The ring matched the jewelry she'd received from Henry for her reward. "This is for you."

"How did you...?"

"Henry said you wanted it to match your reward so he had it couriered from the mainland. I told him a reward was one thing, but the ring wasn't an appropriate gift for a friend to give."

She bit back a smile. "A little territorial, aren't you?"

"You still get the ring, only it's from me, not Henry." Cade removed the ring from the box. "I bought it from him. I'll have the loan paid off by our fiftieth wedding anniversary. Maybe forty if we stick to a budget."

"I don't know anything about budgets, but don't forget I have my own money. My trust fund might not match the Armstrong fortune, but it'll keep a dry roof over our heads, food on the table and Smiling Moon in business for a little while, at least. And if we stick to a budget and clip coupons, it'll last even longer. Of course, no more impromptu purchases such as this ring will be allowed."

His gaze locked with hers. "Is that a yes?"

"Yes." Her heart sang with joy. "You helped me realize so much about myself. I believed I had to marry well because someone else's money would provide the stability, security and sense of belonging I wanted, but money can't give me those things. Love can. You can.

"You're the only person who ever expected something out of me besides looking good and being witty at social gatherings. I wanted to find a man who loved me, but I was so terrified of becoming like my parents and shutting everyone else out, including my own children, that I was afraid to love back. I was afraid to give myself completely to any man."

"And now?" Cade asked.

"It's not all or nothing, like you said. Love isn't exclusive. Love has no boundaries. It's meant to be shared and I have plenty of love to go around for everyone. Especially you.''

He slid the ring onto her finger. A perfect fit. Cynthia expected no less with Henry Davenport involved. No doubt a happy ending was included, but that was something she and Cade would have to work hard to ensure. She was leaving nothing to chance. Or Henry. ''Do you think Henry had this planned all along?''

Cade's smile softened. ''Does it matter?''

''Not right now.'' She stared at the sparkling diamond, sending a colorful spectrum of light around the hospital room. ''But later—''

''Henry came through with a significant donation to Smiling Moon,'' Cade added. ''He didn't have to do that.''

''Yes, he did,'' she said. ''He has no right to play around with people's hearts like this.''

''I'm happy he played around with mine. And yours.'' Cade brushed his lips against hers. Soft, warm and oh-so-Cade. ''I love you, Sterling.''

''I love you, too, Armstrong.''

He laughed. ''So are you ready for your next adventure?''

She smiled. ''As long as you're with me, I'm ready for anything.''

Epilogue

In his library, Henry stared at the pair of gold plated dice in his palm. He would give these to Cynthia and Cade's firstborn as he'd given a similar pair to Noelle Matthews. Henry placed the dice in a velvet pouch and put them in his safe.

Time to get to work. Only ten months until his thirty-fifth birthday. He sat at his desk and opened a file. Party plans were underway, but he had another adventure to dream up. Two more of his friends were going to find a happily ever after together like Brett and Laurel Matthews and the soon-to-be Cade and Cynthia Waters.

Henry tapped his Mont Blanc pen and stared at the guest list. He just had to figure out who was next.

* * * * *

COMING NEXT MONTH

#1666 PREGNANT BY THE BOSS!—Carol Grace
Champagne under the mistletoe had led to more than kisses for tycoon Joe Callaway and his assistant. Unwilling to settle for less than true love, Claudia Madison left him on reluctant feet. Could Joe win Claudia back in time to hear the pitter-patter of new ones?

#1667 BETROTHED TO THE PRINCE—Raye Morgan
Catching the Crown
Sometimes the beautiful princess needed to dump her never-met betrothed—at least that's what independent Tianna Roseanova-Krimorova thought. But a mystery baby, a mistaken identity and a surprisingly sexy prince soon made her wonder if fairy-tale endings weren't so bad after all!

#1668 BEAUTY AND THE BABY—Marie Ferrarella
The Mom Squad
Widowed, broke and pregnant, Lori O'Neill longed for a knight. And along came…*her brother-in-law?* Carson O'Neill had always done the right thing. But the sweet seductress made this Mr. Nice Guy think about being very, very naughty!

#1669 A GIFT FROM THE PAST—Carla Cassidy
Soulmates
Could Joshua McCane and his estranged wife ever agree on anything? But Claire needed his help, so he reluctantly offered his services. Soon, their desire for each other threatened to rage out of control. Was Joshua so sure their love was gone?

#1670 TUTORING TUCKER—Debrah Morris
The headline: "West Texas Oil Field Foreman Brandon Tucker Wins $50 Million, Hires Saucy, Sexy Trust Fund Socialite To Teach Him The Finer Things In Life." The *Finer Things* course study: candlelight kisses, slow, sensual waltzes, velvety soft caresses…

#1671 OOPS…WE'RE MARRIED?—SUSAN LUTE
When career-driven Eleanor Rose wanted to help charity, she wrote a check. She did *not* marry a man who wanted a mother for his son and a comfortable wife for himself. She did *not* become Suzy Homemaker…*nor* give in to seductive glances… or passionate kisses…or fall in love. Or did she?

SRCNM0503